PARKER VALLEY

Jennifer

May God truly Bless you when you come & when you go Go with God

Candace Jane Mann

PARKER VALLEY
SERIES #2

Jennifer

Acknowledgments

To my beloved husband Michael: As each year passes my love for you grows even stronger. You are always there when I need you. Your passion for life keeps my world from spinning out of control. You are my rock and my one and only. Thank you for all the support you have given me as I walk out my dream of catching the stars. We have walked through a journey that would make most people tremble, but because of your steadfast love of our Lord we have journeyed well. You have taught me how to trust and how to love. God gave me at the tender age of 16 a man that most girls only dream of. I look forward to spending the rest of my life in your loving arms and being the whisper of encouragement to your dreams and visions. Thank you, my precious. Without you this would have been impossible.

~

To my daughter Lisa: Lisa I cannot tell you enough how proud I am of you. You have been the wind beneath my wings as I have written this series. Your encouragement and love have not gone unnoticed and I thank you for your loving support. I pray with your wonderful Marcus and my precious grandson Joshua, you will feel God's hand in everything you do, and I thank you for always being there as the strength behind my words. Marcus how I thank you for all you have been to Michael and me, and for loving our daughter as much as you do. You two have planted a flower garden that will flourish and grow with the hand of God's love for you both. Joshua, I can only tell you how delighted God is with you. You bring out the best in everyone you share your heart with. Your heart is pure and God's love will shine forth in all you set your hand to. You will fly with the eagles.

~

To my beloved son Jeff: What a joy it is to see you being molded into the man God has ordained you to be. You have walked through the hardships of life with strength and purpose. You have written a masterpiece with your words and your loving children. God loves a willing heart. Kaitlyn, my precious granddaughter I pray that your sweet spirit will bring joy to all you meet. John, my dear grandson, I hope you know that you light up a room when you walk into it and bring pleasure to the Lord. To my spirited Mary, I pray that God shows you how talented and special you are. Joey, with a heart of gold is a treasure waiting to be opened. My dearest Caleb with the strength of a lion will touch the hearts of all he meets and finally my dearest Madeline, with the plan God has for your life I can hardly wait to see you soar. I am truly a blessed mother and grandmother.

~

To my mother Shirley: Thank you for giving me life in a time of struggle. I am truly blessed to have a mother with such an encouraging spirit. You have been the strength behind my life since the beginning and I love you dearly. I pray that God shows you what a treasure you are for always being there for your four daughters. Growing up with you and dad has been a delight and surprise around every corner. Your delightful nature and your kind heart will forever been inherited by us all. You will live on in our hearts and dreams forever. You are the light of my life. Thank you.

~

To my dear friend Sylvia: Thank you, Sylvia, for being my first editor. You have helped me start a journey that lead to my first series. Your endless hours of editing did not go unnoticed. Thank you.

~

To Gene and Brian: Thank you for the chance to finally see my books published. Gene I thank you for your endless hours of reading something that you were unfamiliar with. You will forever be in my gratitude and my heart.

Chapter One

Jennifer woke up in a cold sweat. Her dream felt so real. She sat up in bed and looked around praying that she was at home in bed and not where her dream reflected. She groaned as she looked around the room and didn't recognize it.

"Oh God, what have I done?" She moaned and lay back down.

Something stirred beside her and a hand reached out and pulled her closer. Jennifer stiffened as she recognized the voice that said,

"Come here, sweetheart. You are one surprising little vixen in bed," he drawled with a delicate southern accent.

"Oh dear God, James, what have we done?" She grimaced. "Get away from me. Oh my head. What have I been drinking?"

"Hush, darling. Come back to bed," James said. His head was groggy.

Shame washed over Jennifer as she remembered small details of last night. How could she have let herself get into that position? Her sisters were going to kill her, and there was no telling how Jason, James's brother, would react. He warned her several times not to get involved with him, but she was her own woman and thought he was being over protective. Her sister Sondra and Jason were still on their honeymoon and would be back in a week's time.

She couldn't remember how she ended up in bed with James but here she was naked beside a man that she wished she had never met. She shuddered again when she felt him touch her in places that made her go crazy. Where did he learn all those things that he did to her? She could only guess at how many women had groveled at his feet and would be delighted to end up in his bed.

When she got up, she looked down and saw blood on the sheets and was sadly reminded of what she had given up to sleep with James.

"Oh God, please forgive me!" she spoke aloud.

James looked down to where she was looking and was shocked to see blood on the sheets.

"Were you a virgin, Jennifer? I wish you had told me. I would have been gentler with you, sweetheart. I'm so sorry. I didn't realize. But I will tell you, I wouldn't have guessed it. You were fantastic." He grabbed her arm and forced her back down and planted an amorous kiss on her neck.

"Stop it, James! How did this ever happen to me? What did you give me to drink last night? My head hurts so badly. Do you have any aspirin?"

James quickly avoided the question because he had given her a small drug in her drink last night. He wanted her to be at ease when he took her to his bed. He wasn't sure that she would have gone willingly.

She got out of bed and ran to the bathroom and was sick just as she reached the toilet. When she came back out, she begged him to take her home. Just as she was about to put her clothes on, she rushed back into the bathroom to vomit again.

James got out of bed and walked over to the bathroom door and asked her if she was alright. He was a little worried that he might have given her too much of the drug in her drink. Her reaction seemed to be quite violent. He wasn't about to tell her what he had done, so he helped her into her clothes and quickly ushered her out of his bedroom and downstairs before anyone could see them.

No one was up when they came down. He practically had to carry her down the stairs because she was so weak. He deposited her in his brother's little black sports car and started to drive her home. He had to stop two times to let her throw up out the door. His guilt showed on his face as he worried about her welfare.

When they arrived at Parker Valley, the ranch that she and her three sisters owned, he helped her up the stairs and into the house. When he had gotten her through the door, he quickly kissed her and left hastily before someone came down and saw them.

Jennifer collapsed on the couch and didn't make it up the stairs before her sister Cassie came down and found her.

"Jennifer sweetheart, are you okay? Have you been down here all night? You look terrible. What's wrong?" Cassie asked, rushing to her side.

"Oh Cassie, I feel terrible. Would you help me to my room? I think I'm going to be sick again," she cried.

Cassie helped her to her room just in time for her to be sick in her bathroom. She was worried about Jennifer and rushed down stairs and called Dr. Martin. He said he would be there within the half hour.

She went back up stairs and confronted her little sister.

"Sweetheart, can you tell me anything? Where have you been? Did you eat something bad?"

"No Cassie, I don't want to talk about it. Please, just leave me alone." She cried into her pillow.

Cassie was not about to leave her sister alone, so she just sat in the chair beside her bed and tried to comfort her with soft prayers. That further shamed Jennifer so she cried even harder.

Claira came into the room and inquired about her.

"I heard Jennifer crying. Is she okay?" she whispered.

"I don't know. I'm a little worried that something has happened to her and she is unwilling to tell us," she whispered back. "I don't think she came home last night. Her bed has not been slept in."

The two left the room and waited for Dr. Martin to come. Twice during that time they heard Jennifer run to the bathroom. They held each other and prayed for their little sister. They were afraid of the worst.

Dr. Martin spent about fifteen minutes in the bedroom with Jennifer and decided that she was dehydrated and needed fluids, so he called for the ambulance to take her to the hospital. She was too weak to argue and the next thing she knew, she was being taken to the hospital.

Cassie went with her and held her hand to try and comfort her.

"Don't leave me, Cassie," she cried, her body shaking all over. They had an IV inserted and she was receiving liquids to regain her strength.

When she arrived at the hospital, she went into the emergency room. She was attended to by two nurses along with Dr. Martin and when they removed her underwear, they noticed the blood stain and other body fluids. They drew blood and took urine samples to try to understand what could possibly have caused such a reaction. One nurse took Dr. Martin aside and inquired about her health.

"I think we should do a rape test. She has all the signs of trauma and victimization."

"Okay, let's get a trauma rape kit in there and find out for sure." Dr. Martin knew the Parker Valley girls all their lives and he worried about their welfare. He was especially concerned for their youngest sister, Jennifer. He too had noticed that she was in shock over something that had happened to her, especially after Cassie had told him that she hadn't come home that night. He felt responsible for her well-being.

Their parents had died in a plane crash less than a year ago and the shock of their loss was still felt among the girls. The oldest daughter, Sondra, a feisty young woman, was married a week ago to a handsome bachelor from Virginia who had recently bought the neighboring property, Willow Oaks. They were the talk of the town. He had come in and rescued the girls from bankruptcy and swept Sondra off her feet. They had a romantic and very quick engagement. The two were deeply in love with each other and were off on their honeymoon to a resort in Northern California. He wondered if he should try and get in touch with Jason, but he decided to wait for the results.

Jennifer was too weak to argue with the nurses when they came in to talk to her and do a physical exam. They took samples and calmly spoke to her, seeing if they could extract any information from her.

Jennifer only groaned and cried that 'God wouldn't be happy with her.'

The nurses looked concerned and tried to reassure her that everything would be alright, but they were firm with her when they took their samples. When they came out of the room they just looked at each other sadly. They spoke to Dr. Martin with their concerns.

Cassie was waiting with Claira in the waiting room. They both tried not to show their fears to one another when Dr. Martin came out to talk with them.

"It seems like Jennifer has had some sexual activity." He tried to explain delicately. "The tests will prove to us if there was any drug use or alcohol use, and possibly the DNA of whoever was involved. I'm sorry girls about the prognosis but the only conclusion I can come up with is an induced drug that would cause her to vomit so frequently. I have seen it before in rape victims. The perpetrator tries to drug the girl into being overly promiscuous so that they will have no resistance when he tries to take advantage of them. I am praying that this is not the case but my best bet is that is what happened." He sadly looked at the sisters and added.

"I'll let you know when we have more conclusive results. Meanwhile, we are sending in a rape counselor to help her overcome this. Are there any questions?"

"Thank you Dr. Martin. When can we go in and see her?" Claira was worried about her little sister.

"Give us at least another half an hour and then we will see how things have progressed. She will need to have her family support at this time. If the outcome is what I think it is, I will be calling the police, but we won't do that until she feels a little better." With a nod he walked out of the room.

"Oh dear God, Cassie, who did she go out with last night? Do you know anything about what is going on and who would do something like that to her?" She cried and threw her arms around Cassie. Together they sobbed and prayed.

Chapter Two

James went home after dropping Jennifer off and went to bed. He himself had too much to drink the night before and needed to sleep it off. He passed Roberta on the way up the stairs and she asked him if he would like to have some breakfast. He refused and said he was going back to bed.

She just shook her head and went about her business complaining that, ever since his brother left for his honeymoon, all James did was party at night and sleep during the day.

"It's none of my business, but he's going to land himself into trouble one of these days," she muttered, wondering who the latest conquest was.

Jason and James's mother and father had left soon after the wedding and went back to Virginia. They were reluctant to leave James behind when their older son was on his honeymoon, but they trusted that he had everything under control and that James would continue to work the ranch the way he had been until Jason and Sondra came home.

Little did they realize that their youngest son took advantage of his position and partied every night.

James went to bed and didn't get up until midafternoon.

The blood tests came back positive for the date rape drug. There were also signs of semen and bruising of the vagina. It appeared to be a definite rape case. When Dr. Martin came back to the girls and confirmed their worst fears, they both were shocked and frightened for their sister.

"I would like to talk to Jennifer if I may. I know she will tell me what has been going on and who it was that raped her. Please, Dr. Martin, let me talk to her! Is she well enough to talk to me?" Her voice was shaking.

"Of course, Cassie, please go in and see if she will talk to you. I will wait until I hear from you whether I should call the police or not."

Cassie told Claira to wait for her and come in a bit later.

Cassie walked down the hallway of the hospital as if it were the last place she would rather be. In her mind she tried to convince herself that this couldn't be happening to her sister but she knew she had to be gentle and understanding. When she opened the door to the room, she peeked in and saw her little sister rolled up in a ball on this large bed with white sheets all around her. She looked so small and frightened. Her hands covered her face and she looked so defeated.

"Hi, Jennifer honey, how are you feeling?" She came into the room and sat on the side of the bed facing her sister.

Jennifer took one look at her and burst out crying.

"Oh Cassie, what have I done? I have disappointed you. I'm so sorry. Will you please forgive me?"

"Oh, sweetheart, you have done nothing wrong. Can you remember anything that happened last night?"

Her sister just looked at her and cried even harder putting her head in her hands.

"I just want to die. Please God, take me home. I miss mom and dad, Cassie. I can't do this alone."

"You are not alone, honey. We are all here for you." Cassie cried with her and just held her until her tears subsided a bit. "What can you tell me, honey? Let's just start at the beginning. Can you remember anything about last night?"

Jennifer looked at her sister with blotchy frightened red eyes and nodded her head yes.

"Why don't you tell me who you went out with and where did you go," she prodded.

Jennifer shook her head no.

"What do you mean no, sweetie? That you don't remember or that you don't want to tell me?" Cassie asked.

"I can't tell you who I went out with but I will tell you where we went." She hiccupped through tears.

"Just tell me anything you want, Jennifer. But eventually you will have to tell someone about what happened and with whom," she encouraged softly. "Why don't you just tell me now and get it all out in the open and then we can deal with it. Okay?"

She still shook her head no.

Cassie was beginning to get frustrated but she kept rubbing her sister's back and tried to coax her to talk.

"Anything you say, sweetheart. Why don't you start at the beginning?"

Jennifer sat up in bed a little more and stared out the window.

"I remember going out to a little restaurant outside of town. I had never been there before but it was nice. I felt so excited and carefree. He treated me like royalty and we laughed and had a great time. Then we got in his car and went to a dance bar outside of Dallas. I had been there before with friends but never alone. I guess I had too much to drink and I began to feel strange." She cried harder when she remembered how she had come on to him.

"I started kissing him, Cassie, and I felt like I couldn't stop. He made me feel so good." She put her hands over her face. "I'm so ashamed. He made me feel things I have never felt before. I just couldn't stop." She cried in gulps.

"We went back to the ranch and he carried me up to his room and that's all I remember. The next thing I do remember is waking up next to him. I felt so awful in my heart and in my body. I started to throw up and I couldn't stop." Jennifer cried harder at that point and said through a shaky voice. "I remember seeing blood on the sheets, Cassie, and I lost it." She put her head on her pillow and stared at the ceiling. "I asked him to take me home and he did."

Cassie tried not to look horrified but she covered her mouth with her hand and listened intently. She began to get a sick feeling in her stomach that she knew the name of the man that she had been with. When Jennifer said he took her back to the ranch it must have been somewhere close by and a familiar place. The only ranch she knew of was Willow Oaks, where Jason's younger brother James lived. She gulped and realized why Jennifer didn't tell her who she was with. She decided to get it out in the open and over with so she came out and asked her.

"Jennifer honey, was it James you were with? Don't be afraid to tell me!" she pleaded.

Jennifer sat up in bed quickly and looked at her sister horrified.

"Cassie, you can't tell a soul. Please, you have to promise me you won't say a word." She started to panic. "I will never forgive you if you tell anyone. Especially please don't tell Jason and Sondra. I don't want to get him into trouble. It was my fault. I must have lured him, Cassie."

Cassie shook her head to try and calm her down. She continued to rub her arm and closed her eyes and prayed silently, asking God to show her what to do.

"Jennifer, it wasn't your fault that this happened to you." She spoke in a reassuring voice. "Do you know anything about the drug 'ecstasy'?"

Jennifer shook her head no.

"You were given that drug last night, Jennifer. It must have been James who gave it to you. It is a 'date rape' drug that makes you do things that you wouldn't ordinarily do. You had that drug in your system when they tested you. You have to tell them it was James that gave it to you. He disrespected you and put your life in danger, Jennifer. You could have died. It made you very sick, sweetheart. You have to make sure that it doesn't happen to anyone else. He also took something from you that was sacred to you. I think you know what I mean."

"Oh Cassie, do you think that God can ever forgive me? I'm so ashamed." She cried harder and harder. "I didn't mean for that to happen. He was surprised that I was a virgin, because of the way I acted." She put her head back in her hands in shame.

"Jennifer, listen to me and listen good. That drug made you do those things. You must not blame yourself or feel any shame. You did not know what you were doing. Look at me!" she demanded a little more harshly.

"I'm very, very angry at James right now. He does not have the right to do things like this to people. He is a very sick man, and should be punished for what he did.

"No, please, I don't want anyone else to know about this. It is a small town and I don't want everyone to know. Please promise me that you won't tell anyone that I told you. I'm so embarrassed. I couldn't take it anymore. Please Cassie, promise me. Especially, don't tell Sondra and Jason. I couldn't face him, because I promised him I wouldn't go out with James. I don't want them to know that I have disappointed them."

"Jennifer, I want you to calm down. James should not be allowed to get away with what he did to you. He needs help, and I want to see that he gets it. He is obviously an angry, confused man that should be whipped for what he did. I believe that Jason is the one who should confront him. After all, he is his brother. He will know how to deal with him. He needs help, Jennifer."

"Oh God, I don't think I could live through that, Cassie. They will always look at me differently."

"That is not true, Jennifer. They know who you are. You are a wonderful young lady who had the misfortune of meeting a man like James. Jason will probably blame himself for his brother's actions. This needs to be confronted as soon as possible. I can either talk to the police or talk to Jason and Sondra. I will leave the decision up to you."

Jennifer cried even harder when she heard that the police may be called in.

"I won't press charges and they can't make me," she said.

"Then we will have to involve Jason and Sondra. I mean this, Jennifer. I cannot keep something like this a secret from them. They are family." She insisted, feeling that this would be the best approach and the least likely to cause a public incident, as much as she would like

James to spend time in jail for what he did to their sister. She would leave it up to them to decide what to do.

"Okay. But no police, please. My shame is big enough at the moment." She turned her head away from Cassie defeated. "Please leave me alone for a while."

Cassie got up slowly and rubbed her back, and left the room quietly.

When she was in the hallway, she put her hands over her face and started to cry. Claira was waiting further down the hall and ran up to her and tried to comfort her.

"Let's go in the waiting room and talk," she said. She quickly took Cassie from the hallway.

"Okay, what did she say?" she asked.

"Oh my God, Claira, it was James who did this to her. She won't allow us to press any charges against him because she doesn't want the publicity. I can't say that I blame her, but I am so angry at him right now. What should we do?"

"The only thing we can do is call Jason and Sondra. They will know what to do," she said.

As the girls went to leave the hospital, Dr. Martin came out of a room and told them he would like to talk to them.

When they entered his office he spoke in a worried tone.

"I spoke to Jennifer and she was not willing to tell me who the perpetrator was. I'm not sure whether I should call the police or not. It is your call. Were you able to get any answers out of her?"

"Yes, and she is not willing to press charges. She knows the man and would like us to handle the incident without involving the police. That does not mean that she won't press charges later. She just wants to see what will happen." Cassie was discouraged with the outcome.

"That's fine with me but please let me know if I can help in any way. We will be sending in a counselor to talk to her this afternoon and then set up some other times they can connect. If we can do anything else, please let us know. We will be releasing her this afternoon around three o'clock. I just want to do some other tests." He looked at them and smiled. "Everything will be okay. Just remember that God is in control."

The girls left the hospital and went back to Parker Valley. Neither one of them spoke on the way home. They were digesting what had happened and what needed to be done. They would call Jason and Sondra on their honeymoon and talk to them and get their advice as soon as they got home. Claira had to go to work soon after their call.

Chapter Three

Jason listened to Cassie on the telephone intently. He groaned inwardly as she told him what had happened to Jennifer. His face turned white when he was told that James was the one who had given her the drug and taken advantage of her.

He was about to slam the phone down hard on the table when Sondra took the receiver and was also enlightened about the horrifying details. She silently cried when Cassie explained the state of mind Jennifer was in.

"Oh my dear God, Cassie, we will be right home as soon as we can get there. Don't worry about anything. Just get Jennifer home in her own bed and we will take care of the situation."

"Dr. Martin wants to inform the police but Jennifer would not tell him what happened to her. She said she would not press charges if they brought the police in. She didn't want to go through the process. I guess in a way I can understand that. Families taking care of their own families, I guess it's the best way to handle things. But, let me tell you, Sondra, if that young man comes into this house I can't be responsible for what I would like to do to him."

"I feel the same way, Cassie. Let us handle things from here. We love you. Thank you for being there. See you soon and all give our love to Jennifer," Sondra said.

Jason paced back and forth in the room while Sondra was on the phone. He was silently praying for wisdom. He ran his hand through his hair and took deep breaths. He kept clenching his fist as if he would like to hit something. Sondra had never seen him so upset. Even when she had caused him so much trouble, he had never looked as distraught.

She remembered at one time that he had said she would never see him in that state but here he was with that look on his face.

"Sondra, what was he thinking?" He paced back and forth. "He could have killed her with that drug." He sat down on the couch and cried with his hands in his face.

Sondra went over to him and put her arms around him.

They had been married for a week and a few days. They went through three months of learning to trust each other with their lives. He had been patient and kind as he taught her the love of the Lord first and his love second. She had become the woman of his dreams when she agreed to be his wife but it was she who still couldn't believe that this wonderful incredible man would want to marry her. When they became one flesh, they became one in the Spirit.

She could feel his pain now and he could feel hers. They cried together and prayed that God would intervene for them.

Jason lied down with Sondra and comforted her. She told him that she would trust anything he wanted to do. They had decided to head back to the ranch and handle the situation with James and Jennifer. He made arrangements with his pilot and driver to pick them up after lunch. They would be home by seven or eight o'clock that evening.

Sondra called Cassie and told her their plans and, when she got off the phone with her, she started to cry. The burdens seem to lift off her shoulders and she could finally let down her guard. Claira had already left for her shop in town and told Cassie that she would help her bring Jennifer home. Cassie agreed to call Claira when she was ready to leave. Cassie wept uncontrollably until all her pent up anger was spent. She didn't realize how much she had relied on Sondra to make decisions around the house. What would she do without her?

It was at that moment that Tommy came into the house and found the love of his life in total anguish. Fear overcame him when he first saw her. Thinking the worst, he asked, 'Who died?' He held her in his arms and waited patiently until she had unburdened herself and told him between tears what had happened.

His face went white and then a terrible anger took over. He was ready to go over to Willow Oaks and beat the stuffing out of James but a better sense prevailed and he stayed to hold his fiancé until she had calmed down.

When he found out that Jason and Sondra were headed home, he felt a little relieved. It would be much better for Jason to handle his brother.

They spent the next few hours praying and consoling each other, until it was time to go to the hospital and bring Jennifer home.

When they arrived at the hospital, Claira met them at the front door of the emergency room. They went into Jennifer's room and found her sitting up, dressed and ready to go. Her eyes were still red but she smiled when she saw her sisters.

Shame burst through her heart when she saw Tommy. She started to tear up and put her hands over her face.

"Oh God, what you must think of me. I'm so sorry to cause you all this much trouble," she cried.

Tommy went over to her and put his arms on her shoulders.

"Jennifer, you have nothing to worry about. We want to get you home so you can get some rest. You have been through enough," he added sadly.

Dr. Martin walked through the door to her room and addressed the family.

"Well, Jennifer, are you ready to go home? Here are your discharge papers. If you will just sign here we will get a wheelchair in here and get you to your car." She signed the papers and Dr. Martin put his hand on her hand. "If you need anything, do not hesitate to call me night or day. Okay?"

"Yes sir. Thank you for all your help," she added weakly.

"You are so welcome, my dear. And don't forget to call Carol Briggs. She has set up an appointment with you in the next week. Jennifer, please don't miss that appointment. It will really help you transition back to normal. You have been through a great deal, my dear, and I have given you something that might make you a little sleepy. My suggestion again is to get some rest." He turned to Cassie and handed her a prescription.

"She can start taking these tomorrow morning for as long as she needs them. The vomiting stopped about four hours ago, so the drug is probably out of her system by now. As far as this prescription goes, you will know when she should stop." He smiled gently and left the room.

The nurse came in and put Jennifer in the wheelchair and wheeled her out to the car. No one spoke as they left and headed for the ranch. Cassie's nerves were almost shot. They were all glad when they reached the ranch and Jennifer was put to bed upstairs. The air was filled with a great spirit of sadness.

~

Jason and Sondra boarded the private jet at three o'clock that afternoon. They had packed up quickly and were chauffeured out of the resort by Jason's driver and taken to the jet in the nearby airport.

Neither one had spoken much since Cassie's phone call. Jason was concerned and Sondra was beside herself with worry. She felt helpless and useless this far away. There were times when anger would well up in Jason and Sondra was worried that he would explode. She had never seen that look on his face before, and was glad that it wasn't directed at her. She had made him angry enough in the past but thank goodness never that intense.

She knew that they would have their moments but Jason was fair and always the gentleman. She wasn't so sure that this time he could keep his anger under control.

She felt that she needed to come up with some options for James. There had to be a reason that James did these terrible things. He was her brother-in-law and was in desperate need of help for his behavior. She had to keep her head, because she was afraid that Jason would just beat the tar out of him and kick him out. That wasn't the answer. He did deserve punishment but it was critical what kind he received. Jail wouldn't be the best option but perhaps there was somewhere he could go to receive help. It wouldn't be optional. He badly needed to be frightened into getting some counseling for his actions.

Sondra remembered a friend of hers in college who went off the deep end with drugs. They sent him somewhere to get help but she couldn't remember where. 'Think, think, think,' she said to herself.

Jason sat beside Sondra on the plane thinking of all the times he had to get James out of trouble. This wasn't the first time he had done something like this, and Jason would make sure it was his last. He was almost afraid of the anger that boiled inside of him. He remembered a girlfriend that had been raped at school, and the beating he gave the culprit. He had been angry then but this was a deeper anger. He loved his brother but could not tolerate him. And he wouldn't allow him to get away with what he did to a sweet innocent girl, especially his new sister-in-law. Just thinking about it made him writhe.

"That's it!" Sondra congratulated herself in remembering the place where people could go and get help. She turned to her husband and looked him in the eye.

"Jason, we could encourage James to go to 'Teen Challenge'. They take on young people like him, even though he is not a teenager, and help them deal with their problems. I had a friend who had gotten into drugs and sex in college and they took him in. He is a changed person. He has come to the Lord in a big way and now serves on the Teen Challenge teams. We could call him when we get home and talk to him," she said. She was excited about her solution.

When she looked at Jason, his mood had not changed. He said nothing to her when she mentioned 'Teen Challenge.' It concerned her that he was so angry because it would not solve any problems and she wanted to help James. She knew it was the enemy trying to destroy their family. She took a deep breath and continued.

"Jason, look at me. It won't solve anything if you go off and use your anger on James. He is just a misguided young man who needs some help. It will only put him further into the enemy's hands if we cast him aside." She hesitated.

"Your parents couldn't handle him either. He needs something more than what has been shown to him. We can help him, Jason. I know that we can." Her voice was quiet.

"The only thing my little brother needs is a good beating and I am just the one to do it. I am sick and tired of cleaning up his messes. This time he will pay for what he has done to Jennifer." He ran his hands through his hair. "Dear God, Sondra, he drugged and raped your sister! What does he have to do to get you to see how disgusting he is? I will not have him near my family anymore. He will not cause us any more problems. I have washed my hands of him. He will be sent away today and I don't want to hear anything more. Do you under-stand?" He spoke firmly.

Sondra could see that she would not have any effect on him at the moment so she kept quiet. But she planned to speak to someone from 'Teen Challenge' as soon as she got home. Jason wasn't thinking clearly so she would have to take the upper hand on this. Whether she liked it or not, James was family and she would do what she could for him. She was upset about what he did but she had to force herself to see past it.

Chapter Four

They landed at the airport at five thirty and a limo was waiting for them to take them to the Parker Valley Ranch.

Jason nodded to his driver and they took off quickly. He had not spoken a word since their last conversation and Sondra was concerned. His anger had not cooled and she feared the worst.

As they drove up to the ranch, Sondra dreaded seeing Jennifer. She felt responsible for her wellbeing and felt that she had let her down. Cassie was waiting for them and hugged both of them and tried not to cry. They went into the house and immediately Jason went upstairs to see Jennifer. Sondra followed right after him. His mood hadn't changed and Sondra was worried that he would cause Jennifer to feel shame and humiliation.

She was sitting up in bed when he knocked on the door. A weak 'come in' came from inside the room and Jason opened the door. When he saw her sitting there forlorn and timid he lost it. He went over to the bed and sat down gently and took her hand.

The look on his face was devastation. He put his head down and whispered to her.

"Jennifer, I am so very sorry that you had to go through what you have been through because of my little brother. Please forgive me, sweetheart. What can I do to help make up for this? I know I asked him to stay away from you but I realize that he can be very persuasive." He ran his hand through his hair again and stood up and paced. "At this moment I am afraid of confronting him because I know I will beat him to a pulp. But Jennifer, make no mistake. He will be punished. I will see to it personally, I promise you. He will never touch you again so you have no fear of that. But I would like to hear from you first. What should we do, sweetheart?"

Jennifer looked at his anguish and the guilt surfaced. She hung her head and could hardly speak. Sondra came into the room and put her arms around her.

"You are going to be just fine, Jennifer. I promise you we will take care of the situation and you will not have to confront James. Jason and I will see that is taken care of, honey, so don't worry." Sondra tried to comfort her.

"Can you tell us what you want us to do? Do you want us to go to the police or handle things ourselves? We need to hear from you first."

"No police, please!" she pleaded. "I couldn't bear it, Sondra. I feel terrible enough already. I'm sorry I disobeyed you, Jason, and went out with James. I had no idea that is why he wanted us to go out together. I really liked him and, God help me, I still do. I thought he liked me too. I'm so ashamed of myself for not listening to you

34

and falling into his trap. Please forgive me." She burst out crying again.

The look on Jason's face tore Sondra's heart to pieces. He was so distraught. She thought he would start to cry. She stepped in and spoke softly.

"There is nothing to forgive, Jennifer. Do not think about it again. What James did to you was uncalled for and we will take care of him. Try your best to forget about it and concentrate on getting well. This too will pass, I promise you. God is so amazing and we will all come through this with Him. Get some rest darling, and we'll see you in the morning." She kissed her on the cheek and tucked her in.

They left the room and shut the door.

"I'm going to kill him!" Jason whispered under his breath.

"Oh Jason, everything will work out. Why don't we spend the night here and speak to James in the morning." She urged, thinking that he will have calmed down by then.

"I know you mean well, Sondra. But don't interfere with what I have to do," he said.

Sondra stopped and put her hands on her hips. "Jason, I know what you are going through and I would like you to take a minute and talk with Cassie and Claira before you do anything rash."

Jason took a deep breath and looked at his new wife.

"I knew there was a reason I married you. You are the sensible one. But Sondra, one day you will come to learn something about me. There are times when I have to do what I have to do. This is one of those times. I want you to stay here. I don't want you involved in this," he stressed to her.

"Jason Alexander Nelson, there is something you will learn about me too. There will be no way that you will go and confront James without me by your side. We are married. You are not a one man band. We are a two-person band. You will have to fight me before I will let you go on your own." She took her stance.

He groaned inwardly. "Please don't make me fight you as well, Sondra, because you will not win."

"You will have to tie me up to keep me from being by your side. We are a husband and wife team and I refuse to let you go without me. I mean it, Jason. And you will have to fight me," she replied with determination in her voice.

He took her by the hand and drew her close to him, and hugged her.

"I don't want you to see what I have to do, Sondra. Can't you understand that?" he whispered in her ear.

"I will not allow you to beat him up, Jason. That would be the wrong approach. He might not even know what he has done? Let's pray about what we should do and then confront him."

He scratched his head in frustration and gave into her. "Okay. Let's go. We will pray on the way," he insisted and ushered her out the door.

Sondra was right. James did not have a clue as to what was happening. He had slept most of the day and got up leisurely and ate dinner by himself on the terrace. He was reading the newspaper when Jason and Sondra came through the door.

Roberta was there to greet them and showed her surprise that they were home so soon.

"Welcome home!" she said, surprised to see them. "Let me put some dinner on for the two of you."

"No thank you, Roberta. In fact, I want you to take the rest of the night off. Go to your room early and we will see you in the morning. Before you go, where is James?"

Roberta looked at Sondra and then at Jason and realized that something was terribly wrong. She pointed towards the terrace and immediately shook her head and nodded in acknowledgement and left the room. She had been with the family long enough to know when to stay out of the way when things got out of control. Sondra realized that was why Jason loved her so much. She smiled weakly and said another prayer.

Jason threw down the suitcases and strode towards the terrace shouting James's name as he went. He was not about to back down now. When Sondra started to follow him he stopped her and told her to stay put.

"Sondra, I love you dearly but I am asking you to stay here," he told her firmly, putting her in a chair.

When she started to get out of the chair, he gave her a look that said 'don't disobey me.' She sat back down and put her hands in her lap. She gulped and prayed for James. She wouldn't want to be him right now.

"James!" he shouted loudly. "Get out here now!"

James looked up from his paper and smiled when he saw his brother. The smile was short lived when he saw the look on his face. He got up from the table with a question on his face.

"Hello, brother dear. You're home early," he said.

"Don't 'brother dear' me, you little creep," he replied. He walked in the room and grabbed him by the collar, and pushed him back.

"Whoa, brother, what's the matter with you?"

"You don't even know do you, little brother?" he said through clenched teeth as he pushed him again this time up against the wall.

"Slow down, what's going on?" He paled as he looked into the dark eyes of his brother.

"Are you going to tell me that you didn't give Jennifer a drug and rape her?" His eyes darkened as he verbalized the words.

James gulped, his eyes got bigger and his face took on a look of fear. His look gave away his guilt and Jason held on to him tighter.

"I thought so," he spoke in a deadly whisper. "There have been times in my life where I would like to have taken a belt to you for the things that you have done and the hurt you have caused mom and dad and others. This goes beyond one of those times and even that would be

38

too good for you right now. I am ashamed to call you my brother." He let go of him before he did something he would regret.

He turned away from him and took a deep breath. That was when he noticed that Sondra had come into the room. She stood there watching him, her eyes glued to his. The look he gave her said that he would deal with her later. His anger overwhelmed him. He didn't like this dark side of himself. If he didn't leave now he would regret it later.

He walked out of the room past Sondra without acknowledging her. She felt his wrath towards her too and she cringed.

She looked at James calmly. He hung his head in shame. The fear of repercussions lay ahead of him. He shrugged his shoulders at Sondra for further explanation.

"Jennifer spent the day in the hospital, James," she spoke in a soft voice. "The drug you gave her did not react well in her system. She is a very sick young lady, and she is lucky to have survived it. If they had not gotten her to the hospital in time that drug would have killed her." She waited for his reaction.

He rubbed his hand through his hair, similar to what Jason did, but there the similarities stopped. He looked remorseful but she still had to get his attention.

"They also did a 'rape kit' in the hospital and took blood and other DNA samples. It was a conclusive test."

James sat down on the chair and covered his face with his hands.

"Dear God! Did they call the police?"

"Do you think that would be a good thing to do, James? Should I advise Jennifer to do that? You would be arrested before the night was out," she challenged. She did not let on to him that Jennifer did not press charges. She did not want him ever to know that fact. She needed leverage to get him some help. Her husband was not thinking clearly at the moment so she would take the upper hand.

"I have asked Jennifer to wait for at least twenty four hours before she calls the police. That will give you enough time to decide what you want to do." She paused and came closer and sat down opposite him.

"Personally, I would like to see you beaten by your brother and put behind bars for what you did to my baby sister but I have another proposition for you. You can either be charged with drug assault and rape and spend eight to ten years in jail or you can go to a place called 'Teen Challenge.' where you will spend at least a year to eighteen months being rehabilitated into being the man that God would have you be. That will be your choice. Jail or 'Teen Challenge,' the choice is up to you and you have twenty four hours to make it."

Sondra got up and left the room leaving James behind to think about what to do. She felt that would give her enough time to research 'Teen Challenge' or come up with an alternative. She then went to look for her husband.

Chapter Five

Sondra went up the stairs to look for her husband and, as she looked around, it hit her that this was now her new home. She had not envisioned her homecoming to be this way but it was what it was. She sighed and thought of Jason's anger towards her as she ascended the stairs to their bedroom.

She only guessed that his room was where she thought it was. She had never been in the master suite before and wondered what it would look like. At the top of the stairs she stopped and looked around. The hallway was long and wide. Pictures of family members graced the walls with oversized elegant frames. The hallway floor was carpeted with a soft beige pile. Her feet sunk down in the deep pile as she walked. She felt like taking her shoes off and let her feet enjoy the luxury of this incredible floor covering.

She giggled as she walked along remembering her visit to his sister's room where she had showered and changed after her excursion on the range when Sasha, her horse, had thrown her. Jason had carried her up to the room and deposited her in his sister's room as if she was a nuisance to be dealt with. She had learned the hard way to be a gracious guest in Jason's home.

But she loved it here. The halls were filled with a loving and kind spirit of generosity and friendship. She could hardly comprehend that Willow Oaks would be her home where she would grace its rooms and entertain its guests. She prayed that she would live up to Jason's expectations.

When she peaked in the door of the master bedroom, she saw Jason standing at the window looking out over the pastures. She watched him gaze out the window and wondered what he was thinking. The love she shared for him filled her heart with great joy. She knew that she had gone against his wishes and was ready to pay the consequences. He could be harsh but always fair.

Before she could speak, he turned around and saw her standing in the doorway. His face lit up when he saw her and all the stress of the day disappeared. He walked over to her and smiled.

"I know this is not much of a welcome, Sondra, but welcome to your new home anyway. This is not the homecoming I had planned but here we are, Mrs. Nelson. I love you so much." He sighed and swung her up in his arms.

"Let's deal with what just happened later, okay?" He shut the bedroom door and carried her to his bed. "Welcome home, darling."

~

James paced back and forth. He had never seen his brother so angry. He was worried that he would do something drastic. He sat down and put his hands over his face.

He thought about last night and what he did. He had done it only once before and the girl had been very willing. He had thought that perhaps Jennifer would have been a little more challenging to woo into his bed and that was when he decided he would help things along. It worked before and it certainly had worked this time too.

He shook his head in memory of the blood on the sheets. She had been a virgin. That had taken him completely by surprise because of her aggressiveness the night before. The drug must have had a strong effect on her. He regretted the impulsiveness of giving it to her, especially since she was his sister-in-law's sister.

"What was I thinking? Dear God, I might have killed her!" he spoke out loud. He stood up and paced again.

"I have to get out of here." He panicked. She would have every right to call the police. "Stupid." He kicked himself.

He snuck upstairs and slipped into his bedroom. It was a large spacious room with a king size canopy bed. 'More of a chicks room' he thought when he first saw it. But he wasn't going to complain. He was glad to have a roof over his head.

His parents had given him a good size allowance but he spent most of it on clothes, parties and girls. When they took his allowance away after the last incident with a girl in Virginia, he was in need of a place to hang out, and some money to do it with. His brother offered him an alternative.

He loved his brother but hated his superior attitude when it came to rules and regulations. Working the ranch was a job that he didn't mind as long as his nights and weekends were free. They had set up a great arrangement here in Texas. His brother had no idea what he did at night or on the weekends. He told him as long as he was up by six o'clock and put in a full day's work he could do anything he wanted on his off time. That suited James's lifestyle just fine. So far, he had stayed out of trouble.

He should have known that Jennifer would be trouble. She was far too innocent for his tastes. He never varied from his type of woman and couldn't believe that he had made that mistake. But she was beautiful and had an independent air about her. He liked her spunkiness and her playful attitude. She had led him to believe that she was experienced with men with her flirting and the way she talked. She was like a lioness that needed to be tamed and he was going to be the one to do it.

He kicked himself again for making the wrong decision with the wrong woman. He had to be out of his mind.

He pulled out his suitcase and started packing his clothes and belongings. He could be out of here in no time. Fear gripped him as he pictured himself behind bars. Sex offenders did not do well in prison.

He slipped out the door quietly and jumped in the extra vehicle that was tucked away in the garage. He would leave it at the parking garage at the airport and tell Jason later where he had parked it. He felt he was lucky enough to escape. Where he would go would be another question, and one he would decide when he got to the airport. Perhaps Jamaica would be nice this time of year.

No one heard him leave that evening. It wasn't until morning that it was discovered that he was gone. A note was left in his bedroom that told them he was very sorry for all the trouble he had caused them and to please tell Jennifer that he was sorry for what he had done. He really did care for her, and he hoped she would forgive him and that they could eventually be friends.

When Jason read the letter he crumpled it up in one hand. Sondra had come in the room looked at him with a question in her eyes. Jason was furious. He looked at her with an accusatory look and shook his head.

"What did you say to him when I left the room last night?" he barked at her.

"I don't know what you are talking about. Are you saying that I am the cause of his leaving? Be careful what you say, Jason."

"Sondra, I'm not accusing you of anything." He took a long breath. "I just want to know what you said that may have caused him to leave. I'm just curious."

"I gave him an ultimatum," she admitted.

"What kind of ultimatum did you make, Sondra?" His patience was waning and he ran his hand through his hair. "I don't know how to ask you any clearer, without sounding trite."

"I'm sorry, Jason, if I overstepped my place. I thought he should know he had a way out. I told him it was either jail, or Teen Challenge." She gave him a sheepish look. "I'm sorry I did that without consulting you first but I really thought that he would take me up on it. I'm so sorry, darling. Please forgive me?"

Jason paced the room and looked like he was about to have an angry outburst. But he stopped and looked at her with a defeated expression.

"I know you were just trying to help. But I did ask you to stay out of this last night. The reason I didn't address it last night, was because I didn't want James to see us at odds with each other, and it was our first night in our home together. I didn't want anything to destroy that for us. If I had known what you were going to say to him, things might have been different." He paced the room while he spoke.

"I know my brother very well, Sondra, and I could have guessed what he was going to do. He is basically a weak man. He would choose any alternative to going to jail and it would take a miracle for you to get him to go to Teen Challenge."

Sondra looked completely out of her comfort zone.

Jason went over to her and put his arms around her.

"Honey, please do not do anything like that without talking to me first. Can we please agree on that?" he asked.

"I'm sorry, Jason. I so wanted him to agree to go. It would change his life." She cried softly. "What are we going to do?"

He continued to hold her and replied tenderly. "Let's pray and find out what God wants us to do, okay — I know we will come up with something."

Sondra was so moved by his tenderness that she submitted to his counsel. He prayed with a gentleness that only came from the Father. The two of them stood together holding each other and prayed fervently for James, and what their part would be in his future.

~

Meanwhile, James had made it to the airport and was about to board the American Airlines Jet, taking him, first class, to Miami and then on to St. Croix, where he could relax and think about what he should do next, when he noticed two police officers come up to the counter. Perspiration began to form on his upper lip and fear gripped his heart.

The police officers looked around when the gate attendant pointed to the people sitting in the waiting room. He started to panic when they came forward and asked the gentleman sitting next to him to come with them. His heart pounded in his chest and he could hardly breathe. He knew if he looked in the mirror his face would be white as a sheet. He thought for sure that they were coming for him.

He gulped and breathed a sigh of relief.

'Dear God, what am I doing? Will I be looking over my shoulder wondering when they would come after me?' he thought to himself.

He had a bout of guilt and thought he should call his brother and turn himself over to him. What could be worse, running from the law or face his brother and his punishment? He got up and walked around wrestling with himself. When he looked up and saw the man taken away in handcuffs his mind was made up. He pulled out his cell phone and called Jason.

Jason answered the phone and James was silent. Finally he spoke.

"Jason, this is James. I'm at the airport on my way to Miami and then on to St. Croix. I want to make things right with you and Jennifer. I am going to come back so that we can talk. Would that be okay?" His voice sounded defeated.

"James, I'm so glad you called. I knew you would make the right decision, brother. Actually if you look over your right shoulder you will see me. I am here at the airport praying that you would call."

"Are you kidding me? Where are you?" He looked around and finally saw him. He knew then that his decision to call Jason was the best decision he had made in a long time.

Jason went up to his brother and hugged him.

"Welcome home, James. At least now I know we can now help you. I was worried that you would board that plane."

"I had a little help making my decision, with that man next to me being arrested. I felt like I would be looking over my shoulder for the rest of my life. I couldn't live that way. Jason, I made a big mistake and I know I have to make it right." His eyes had tears in them when he looked at his brother. He was quite shaken.

"I have a confession to make also, James. That man was not really arrested. He is an actor and so were the policemen. I was desperate to make you understand the decision you were making and I was hoping you would see what you would be faced with and what you were running from. Will you forgive me for forcing the issue?"

"Are you serious? I thought for sure they were coming for me. That was a pretty good act and it really made an impression on me. I guess I should thank you for going to all that trouble," he admitted reluctantly. "You are a crazy brother but I do love you."

"It was really Sondra's idea. She has a lot of faith in you, James. She thinks you're redeemable. And to be honest with you, I do too."

They left the airport and rode home together. Jason would have the car picked up later.

Chapter Six

Sondra waited patiently at home praying that James would come home. She knew that Jason loved his brother and had been praying for him to grow up and make some good decisions. It was for that reason Sondra wanted James to go to Teen Challenge and face his concerns and start living a more responsible life. She loved the way her husband cared for his family. They wanted nothing more than for James to become the man that God intended for him to be.

Hoping he would make the proper decision, she had called all around to her friends and acquaintances about Teen Challenge. When she had been given some names of people to contact she called them directly. There were open spaces coming up in the next week when James could enroll. He had to meet certain criteria but Sondra was sure that he would be accepted, especially if Jason was to use his persuasion.

When Jason called her from his cell phone, she cried. They were coming home. Now they could start to build a trust that would be a good foundation from which to start. Her prayers were answered. When she got off the phone she raised her hand and shouted, "Yes Lord!"

She paced the room until they opened the door and she ran directly into Jason's arms.

"Oh Jason, I'm so happy." She turned toward a sheepish James and smiled. "And I am very proud of you, James." She hugged him too.

"Let's go sit down and have a little talk," Jason said to his brother, leading the way. "Sondra, please come and join us. You should hear this too."

Jason was glad that his brother had made the first step but he knew that it was only the beginning. He would have to be strict and unrelenting with him. It was the only thing that he understood. As long as there were ultimatums, he would respond. If they were too soft he would not take the high road. He would take the easy road. And Jason was still angry enough not to let him off the hook that easily.

When they sat down, he looked his brother directly in the eye and asked him what he wanted to do. He had to hear it from him first before he would do anything to help him. James would have to ask for help. The other way around would only make them appear weak, and it wouldn't help James.

James squirmed in his chair. He looked forlorn and lost.

"I don't know what to do, Jason. I feel terrible that Jennifer had such a terrible reaction to the drug I gave her. I'm so sorry I gave her anything. I don't know what

I was thinking." He shook his head. He stood up and began to pace.

"I want to change and I want to do the right thing. I just don't know what it is. I've been a screw up my whole life."

Jason watched his brother and tried to figure out his true motive. It was a good start that he wanted to change and it was even better that he was sorry for what he had done. It was up to him whether the change was real or not.

Sondra piped up and spoke:

"I talked to someone from Teen Challenge and there is an opening that will come up next week. You will have to meet their criteria but I'm sure that won't be a problem. Does that sound like something you would consider doing?"

James looked at her with a frown on his face.

"I really don't know anything about it. Is it a lock down situation?" He sat down by Sondra.

"Not exactly. You can have visitors now and then, but they want to be in complete control of where you go and what you do." She spoke softly to him. "If you were to run after being admitted you would likely go to jail.

"I don't know if I can be in that kind of environment," he replied

"Listen to me, brother." Jason spoke up, barely keeping his voice in control. "You don't have a choice. You made a very bad mistake yesterday. Jennifer's life has been changed forever and you are responsible for that.

There are consequences to pay. You disrespected and took advantage of her vulnerability and almost killed her. She was an innocent child, James, and you took that innocence and destroyed it. Women look to us men for respect and guidance not lust and control. You not only broke the law, James, you took my new sister in law and stole her virginity without her consent. Look at the alternative you face — a nice small cold jail cell. Rapists don't do very well in jail, James." Jason's voice became louder when he spoke, anger starting to rise to the surface again, as he remembered what his brother had done.

"Like I said earlier, you are lucky I don't beat the stuffing out of you and that Jennifer has held off calling the police." He stood and paced again.

"Okay." James paused and took a deep breath. "Let's do it." He put his head in his hands.

"I'm so ashamed of what I did to Jennifer. The thing about it is that I really like her. I guess I was trying too hard for her to get to like me too." He looked up at Sondra. "Can you ever forgive me?"

Sondra looked at James and smiled weakly.

"I wasn't sure at first, James, but of course, I forgive you. It's God you need to take your case to and then I guess to Jennifer, if she'll listen to you. I pray that you take this seriously because it may be the only chance you will get."

"Okay, let's do it before I change my mind," he answered faintly, a sudden fear creeping in.

Jason got up and shook his hand and told him how proud he was of him, and that they were there for him if he ever needed them.

"One thing I will insist on and that is you will have no communication with Jennifer. Is that clear brother?"

"Yes, Jason, but I wish I could have the chance to tell her how sorry I am. The truth is that I really like her. I wish I could take that night back." He sighed with regret.

"I know, James, I do too. Now let's get something to eat." He spoke a little louder knowing that there were ears listening. "Roberta, I know you are there listening. We're ready for you whenever you are."

Roberta just shook her head and appeared out of nowhere.

"I was just interested in knowing when you all were going to have some lunch," she added, with her nose out of joint for eavesdropping. "Lunch is served." She smiled and winked at Jason and walked into the kitchen. "You made the right decision, James." She walked back to the kitchen.

~

The next few days went by quickly. James was enrolled in the 'Teen Challenge Program' that was closest to Dallas. He was put through some grueling questions but was finally accepted. It helped that Jason used considerable persuasion to convince them to take on his brother. He spent the last few days researching the program and was very impressed with their results. He had to admit that Sondra was absolutely right because it looked like a perfect fit for James.

Jason had called his mother and father and filled them in on what was going on. His father was very distraught over what James had done and his mother too was beside herself with grief. They promised to pray for them. They were, however, delighted to hear James had agreed to make the decision to finally get some help. They couldn't think of a better place for him. They spoke to Sondra and shared their disappointment with James and told her to give Jennifer their love. They would do anything to help in the situation if only they knew how.

Sondra encouraged them to pray and seek the wisdom of God in their plans to help Jennifer recover from her ordeal.

Sondra spent the next week with Jennifer. She was depressed and wouldn't leave her bed. She was beside herself to know how to help her. Doctor Martin told her not to worry as the drugs he had given her would make her sleepy and calm her nerves. He told her they could stop the drugs at any time and she would very quickly perk up.

That was the case after the third day. Jennifer came down for breakfast and Cassie was delighted. She made her some of her favorite blueberry pancakes. It was good to have their little sister back again.

Jennifer still felt a little awkward with her sisters but slowly overcame her embarrassment. Her counselor, Carol Briggs, had called last night and encouraged her to keep her appointment with her that week. Jennifer was shy about agreeing to meet with her but she really wanted everything to go away, and knew that Carol would hound her until she said yes. She agreed to meet the next day. That seemed to settle Jennifer's spirit a little. 'Perhaps everything would be okay,' she thought to herself.

That night, Jennifer had a strange dream. She dreamt she was walking through a gate into a grave yard. She wandered around not knowing what she was looking for when all of a sudden two people approached her from a distance. They were women with beautiful long dark hair that flowed down and covered their bodies. When Jennifer looked a little closer she noticed that they were not wearing any clothes. Their skin was as white as snow. They frightened her but she kept walking towards them. It was then that she noticed there was blood streaming down their legs. She looked into their faces and tears flowed from their eyes as they looked at her accusingly. They stretched out their arms and tried to grab her. She ran away and started screaming. She woke up suddenly with the scream still on her lips and her heart beating fast.

"Jennifer honey, it's alright. I am right here." Cassie sat on her bed and held her little sister. "You were just having a bad dream. It's okay." She gently rocked her until she stopped shaking.

"Cassie, that dream was so real. I'm so frightened. Would you stay with me please?" Tears streamed down her face. "I hate that I am such a baby."

"It's alright, sweetheart. It was just a dream. No one will hurt you. I promise you."

They spent the night sleeping together with Cassie praying fervently for her sister and keeping an ear out for any more bad dreams but the night was peaceful.

Her appointment day came quickly and Jennifer drove into town to meet with Carol Briggs. Her office was small but delicately decorated to suit the lovely woman with short gray hair. She was in her mid-sixties and had a motherly air about her. When she saw Jennifer, she gave her a gentle hug and ushered her into her office.

"Come in, my dear. Please excuse the mess. I am moving to a larger office where there will be more room to move around. Please make yourself comfortable. Can I get you anything to drink?" Jennifer shyly declined.

"Now, my dear, tell me all about you. My friend Doctor Martin told me how wonderful you were and I could hardly wait to meet you. He didn't tell me how beautiful you were," she complimented sweetly.

"Thank you for the compliment, ma'am," she answered.

"Before we start, I want you to feel comfortable to talk about anything you like. You are safe here. But first, would you mind if I said a little prayer?" she asked.

Jennifer shook her head.

"Father, I want to thank you for bringing Jennifer here safely today. Please come and visit with us, and I pray that you open doors to your heavenly kingdom and give us clear visions as to what your purpose is. Unlock the doors the enemy would keep shut, and let your light shine through. It is in the precious name and blood of Jesus that I pray. Amen." She smiled at Jennifer and sat back and relaxed against her chair.

"So, my dear, tell me about what's going on." Her eyes were kind and Jennifer started to relax.

"I'm not really sure what's going on. I have been through a very painful and embarrassing experience, and I would just as soon forget all about it." She spoke bravely, not sure what was expected of her.

"Would you like to tell me about it? Sometimes it is good just to talk it out with someone who isn't involved."

"Well to begin with I have three sisters that are very possessive and don't think I am capable of doing anything on my own. My parents died in a plane crash nine months ago and last weekend the boy who I trusted raped me," she blurted out angrily, trying to shock her.

"My, you have been through a lot haven't you, Jennifer? Tell me, what bothers you the most — your sisters' bossiness, your parents dying, or you being raped?" she asked without batting an eye.

Jennifer looked at her as if she had horns on her head. She laughed out loud and said,

"Nothing shocks you does it?"

"My dear, there is nothing you could tell me that I haven't heard yet. In fact, I have heard a lot worse. But what is important is that you think it is horrific and it certainly is. Losing one's parents is a tragic event. Being raped is a tragedy all on its own because it is very personal. Why don't you tell me about that first?"

Jennifer caught her breath and suddenly she felt comfortable talking with this woman. She felt like she would understand what she was feeling.

"I went out on a date with my new brother-in-law's younger brother, James. He reminded me very much of Jason, who is my brother-in-law." Her mouth curved with a hint of a tender smile.

That smile was not lost on Carol but she would tackle that later.

"Jason didn't want me to go out with his brother, but James was too persuasive to resist. We went for dinner and then he took me to a bar for drinks and then we went back to his place and I don't remember much from that point on." She tried holding back her tears.

"Don't be afraid, Jennifer. Tell me how you felt in his presence."

"I liked him a lot. He is about four years older than me and far more experienced. I was afraid that he would think I was a baby, if I didn't go along with him. He flirted and made me feel special. I haven't gone to many bars because I am only eighteen, and my sisters would kill me."

"Tell me how he made you feel special?" Carol tried to prod further.

"He liked the way I walked and carried myself. He thought I was older than I looked. They didn't even ask me for my identification at the door of the bar. That I found very strange. Maybe because I was with James and he gave a big tip to the door man."

"So James was extravagant when he took you out?" she asked.

"Yes, he threw money around like it was water. He was tipping everyone big bucks, even the waitress. He flirted with her too. They treated us like gold and I felt pleasure being by his side. I know I had too much to drink that night and my sisters have told me that he put something in my drink to make me more 'amorous.'" She stopped and put her face in her hands.

"Take your time, Jennifer. It is always hard to go through the facts but it is also very healing. Did he make you feel things that you didn't expect?" she whispered.

"Oh God, I don't understand it myself. He touched me in places where I felt like my skin was on fire. And that was at the club. When we left, I could hardly wait for him to touch me some more. I am a terrible person, Miss Briggs. I feel like a whore." She cried with tears streaming down her face. "He and I did things to each other that make my skin crawl. I am so ashamed and embarrassed. God hates me I'm sure for the things I have done."

Jennifer sobbed uncontrollably and Carol handed her some Kleenex to wipe her eyes. She looked at her with sympathy but she let her cry it out. As soon as she had calmed down a bit, she faced her gently.

"Do you know anything about the drug ecstasy?"

Jennifer shook her head no.

"It is a drug known to cause a person to 'loosen up' or have 'no inhibitions.' It is a very dangerous drug because it can be used to lure young women into doing things they wouldn't normally do. It allows your mind to do strange things. This drug was given to you, Jennifer. Under its influence, you did things that were not normal for your personality. You had no control over your body or what you did. It was a very cruel thing that was done to you. Do you understand what I am saying?" She wanted to be clear that Jennifer understood what she was saying.

"I think so. But I remember the feelings like yesterday. Sometimes my body betrays me and I feel things." She looked at her horrified.

"I know, darling. You are a woman who has experienced feelings that married women in love feel. It is natural for them to experience what you experienced. The only difference with you is that it wasn't in God's timing for you to have those feelings before you met the man you would fall in love with and marry. There is nothing wrong with feeling those wonderful feelings under the right circumstances, except it was under the influence of drugs. The drug you were given intensified the womanly parts of your body and those feelings became more intense and unnatural." She sat up and reached for Jennifer's hands. "I want you to do something for me. I want you to pray and ask God for forgiveness. Would you like to do that?" She looked intently into her eyes.

Jennifer nodded yes.

"Jennifer, I want you to repeat after me. 'Father, forgive me, for allowing myself to be in the position I was in last weekend.'" Jennifer repeated the words with her eyes closed. "Father, forgive me for not being obedient, by not listening to Jason and going out with James." She repeated the words. Carol's words became gentler. "Father, I forgive James." She repeated reluctantly, "For giving me the drug and taking advantage of my body and hurting me by taking away something that was precious to me." Jennifer hesitated but finally repeated the words. "I ask you now, Lord, to make my body new again and give me back what was lost to me." Jennifer began to cry as she repeated the words.

Carol waited for a minute before going on. "Now Father, I release James into your hands to do with what you will." Jennifer repeated the words. "I ask you this and thank you, in the name of Jesus. Amen." She paused. "Now take a deep breath and blow it out."

Jennifer continued to cry. "Do you really think the Lord has forgiven me for what I have done?"

"What do you believe?" She spoke softly looking deeply into her eyes. Jennifer nodded yes. Carol's eyes narrowed seriously and she said,

"We serve a loving Father, Jennifer, one who loves His children beyond imagination. When we ask for forgiveness with a repentant heart, He always gives it. Sometimes it comes with consequences and sometimes not. The next step is to forgive yourself. Would you do that with me?" Jennifer nodded yes.

"Father, I forgive myself for being in the position of being hurt." She repeated. "I ask you to heal my heart, my soul, and my mind and my body. Amen."

"Tell me, how you are feeling now?" She smiled.

"Much better, thank you!" She gave her a big smile. "I didn't realize that I was holding so much anger towards James and myself. But I'm beginning to finally feel free."

Carol laughed and gave her a hug. "Let's pray before I send you home. Father, what a delight it is to pray for this special young lady. I pray that you keep her in your loving arms and comfort her when she needs comforting. Be with her when she goes forth and help her to put the past behind her. I thank you, Jesus, for your loving kindness and for allowing us to share intimate thoughts together. Amen."

"I appreciate you taking the time to see me. Can I come back and talk with you some more?"

"My office will always be open to you, my dear. Please take some time alone and begin to read more scripture and go into your prayer closet and seek God's plan for your life." She stopped and looked at Jennifer carefully. "I believe that He has something important for you to do. I feel the Lord wants you to know that you will change the lives of many." She looked at Jennifer puzzled. "I'm not sure I know what that means but whatever happens I want you to trust God. Will you promise me that?" She looked at her seriously.

"I will try," she promised.

After Jennifer left the office, Carol called over to Doctor Martin's office. He took the call as soon as he knew it was her.

"Carol, what can I do for you?"

"I've just spoken to Jennifer. It seems that she is doing fine. She is a sweet girl and I am glad to be able to help her see her way out of this." She paused and took a deep breath. "I am concerned about one thing and I want you to think about this. I believe that she is going to be facing some new challenges. I'm not sure what but I want you to keep your eyes open and let me know if there are any changes in her health. Do you suppose this encounter could result in a pregnancy? It's just a guess, but something tells me we should check it out." She sounded concerned.

He took a deep breath. "Wow Carol, is that your discernment? I hadn't even considered that possibility but it is a very good question. I will have her come in today and we will do a test." He sounded sad. "I hope you are wrong."

"So do I, Charles. So do I," she replied.

Chapter Seven

Days turned into weeks before James was accepted into the Teen Challenge program. The night before he was to leave, he became restless. He knew that the next year would be a year of changes to his lifestyle. He paced in his room thinking about Jennifer. 'I would love to see her and ask her to forgive me,' he thought as he paced. He looked at his watch and saw that it was seven thirty. This would be his only chance to see her for a whole year. He wanted her to know that he liked her very much and to ask if there was a chance after his time at Teen Challenge she would consider seeing him again.

Could he risk the wrath of Jason and go and see her? 'Perhaps I could call,' he wondered, convincing himself it was the right thing to do. He picked up the phone and dialed the number of the Parker Valley Ranch. Cassie picked up the phone.

"Hello?" she said.

"Hello, Cassie? Please don't hang up. I was hoping to speak to Jennifer before I left in the morning. I only wanted to apologize to her for what I did. Could you please let me talk to her?"

Cassie took a deep breath and replied. "I don't think that is a very good idea, James. Jason wouldn't approve. Jennifer is just starting to come around and I don't want anything to set her back. I hope you understand, but the answer is no. We will be praying for you while you are away. I think you made a good choice and we are proud of you, James, but let's just leave this alone." She hung up the phone.

James paced the room again feeling more and more depressed. He had to talk to her. It almost became an obsession. He lay down on the bed and thought of all the times he had manipulated others. He really wanted to make this up to Jennifer. He just couldn't leave without addressing these unsettled matters.

The house was quiet when he went down stairs, hoping to speak to Jason. But he and Sondra had gone to their room. He looked around and made the decision to ride over to Parker Valley and see Jennifer. He had to see her tonight as tomorrow it would be too late.

He drove out of the driveway quietly but unbeknownst to him Jason was watching from the window.

'What is that kid up to?' he thought. Sondra came out of the bathroom and asked what was wrong.

"James has left the building," he announced with a disgusted look on his face. I had a feeling that he would somehow manage to wheedle out of his deal. I should have known." He hit his fist in his palm. "I should have beaten the stuffing out of him when I had the chance."

"Now Jason, let's think this out thoroughly. What was the last conversation you had with him?"

66

"Sondra, I don't have time to analyze the situation. I have to go after him." He started putting his pants on.

"Wait, Jason. I think he talked to you about visiting Jennifer before he left. Perhaps he went over to the ranch to see her."

"You have much more faith in him than I do. But I will call over there just in case and put them on alert." He reached for the phone.

"Would it be so terrible for him to talk to her before he leaves tomorrow? What can it hurt? He has changed a lot, Jason, and I believe it would be good for Jennifer to have him apologize to her. It would be very healing."

Jason stopped for a moment before dialing the number.

"You might have a point, darling. What made you so smart? I'm glad I am married to you. What would I do without you?" He bent over and kissed her on the lips. "Umm you smell so good." Sondra laughed and pushed him away.

"Get on with your call. He should be there soon." Sondra prayed that he was on his way to Parker Valley and not taking off. She felt she got to know the real James the last few weeks. They had many conversations and Sondra felt like it wouldn't take long for him to turn around his life.

~

Cassie and Claira waited for James to come to the ranch. After the call Cassie had earlier from James, they were sure that he would be here.

"Claira, I'm not sure whether it is such a good idea for James to talk to Jennifer. She has come such a long way and I would hate to see her have a setback. Perhaps just seeing James will send her into a frightened spell. I'm not prepared to risk that. She has been through enough already. It might ease his mind but if it causes Jennifer any grief it won't be worth it," Cassie said.

"I know how you feel, Cassie, but somehow we just have to trust God in some situations. It might be just what the doctor ordered. Sondra did say that he had changed a lot in the past couple of weeks and he is very remorseful. The least we can do is wait and see what happens," Claira said.

Neither of the girls heard his car come up the driveway. He parked it down the lane and walked the rest of the way. He figured out where Jennifer's room was and threw a stone gently and it clinked against the glass. When nothing happened he threw another one.

After a few minutes he saw the curtain open and Jennifer peered out into the night. She looked so frightened that James was unsure whether he should show himself. She caught sight of him and opened her window.

"What are you doing here?" she whispered down to him.

"I need to talk to you. I can't leave without saying I'm sorry and saying goodbye. Can you come down and talk to me please, Jennifer. I really need to see you."

He heard the window close and saw the curtains drawn. He didn't know if he had gotten through to her. He patiently stood waiting for some sign of life. The back door opened and Jennifer stood there and motioned for him to come up.

James was happy that she had agreed to meet with him and he carefully made his way up the back stairs.

"Hello, Jennifer. I'm so very sorry that all this happened to you. Please, please, forgive me for putting you through all this pain. I couldn't leave without telling you that and saying goodbye to you. I'm really sorry. I will spend the rest of my life trying to make it up to you, I promise." He hung his head shamefully.

"There were times when I hated you, James, and then there were times that I couldn't get you out of my head. I think that it is good that you are going into a program where they can help you. But you must be willing to receive that help in order for it to be successful. Are you ready to receive help?" She gave him a slight smile.

"I think so. I'm ready to change because of what I did to you. It made me realize what kind of terrible person I was. Please forgive me. I couldn't live with myself if I knew you still hated me. I really like you and I think you are an amazing woman. I guess in a way I didn't feel good enough for you. It's a flimsy excuse and it doesn't make up for what I did. I just wanted you to know. Will you write to me sometime?" His big blue eyes were begging her to respond.

"I will write to you, James. And yes, I forgive you."

"Thank you, Jennifer. And please pray for me because I'm going to need it." He took a deep breath and turned to leave.

"I will pray for you, James. And will you please pray for me too?" She went back upstairs.

Jennifer was on her way up the stairs when she ran into Cassie.

"Jennifer, what are you doing up?" She was surprised to see her.

"I was just talking to James at the back door." When she saw the look that Cassie gave her, she put up her hand. "He was a gentleman and just wanted to apologize for his behavior and say goodbye. It was all very innocent, so don't look at me with those accusing eyes."

"I would never accuse you of anything, Jennifer. I'm surprised that would come from you. Do you think that I blame you for what happened?"

"I don't know, Cassie. I feel like no one trusts me anymore. I'm tired all the time and I don't feel very well. I think it is this place. It is depressing me. All I think about is Mom and Dad. I miss them so much. I should probably go back to school on Monday. Gayle has been calling me and filling me in on what is going on. I have been keeping up with my studies, but I think I would like to go back." She told her, resigned to her plan.

Cassie looked at her sister with worried eyes. "Are you sure it is not too soon for you?"

"No Cassie, I think I will be just fine. I might start feeling a little better in a different atmosphere. Doctor

70

Martin took some more blood today for another blood test. I assume it is to make sure the drug is out of my system so as soon as I hear the results I want to drive back to school."

"Okay, Jennifer. Let me talk it over with Sondra and Jason and see what they say."

"Forget about what they say. It is my life and I want to live it my way. I am going back to school and that is final." She left Cassie standing there and went upstairs to her room and slammed the door.

Cassie stared after her sister, wanting to go up there and give her a piece of her mind. Claira came up to her and put a hand on her shoulder.

"Let her do what she wants. She is a grown woman now and we are going to have to let her go. All we can do is pray for her, Cassie. Are you going to call Sondra or shall I?"

Cassie pursed her lips together, still angry at her sister for dismissing her. 'I try to do the best for her and she snubs me for it,' she thought to herself.

She called Sondra and filled her in on what transpired with James and Jennifer, trying to keep the concern and annoyance out of her voice. She didn't want to sound like she wanted to control her but when she told her about going back to school Sondra agreed wholeheartedly. Cassie's annoyance continued, now annoyed with Sondra for agreeing with Jennifer.

It was at that moment that Cassie washed her hands of the whole episode. 'Let her make her own mistakes.

I'll be there to pick up the pieces,' she ranted to herself, as she made her way up to bed.

~

James left later the next morning to go to an undisclosed place where he would be part of Teen Challenge for one year to eighteen months. He had promised his brother that he would stick it out for at least the one year to see what would happen. He was determined to change his life and his lifestyle. They picked him up and they all said their teary goodbyes.

"I will be praying continuously for you, James," Sondra said as she hugged him.

Jason hugged his brother also and told him how proud he was of him. He looked a bit frightened and worried about what to expect.

"I'll keep in touch. Say goodbye to everyone for me. I hope that you both get a chance to visit me." He was worried that he would lose touch with his family.

"Don't you worry, my brother. We will be there as often as they allow us to be. You take care of yourself and stay clean. I'm counting on you." He slapped him on the back. "See you soon."

James got into the transportation van and gave them one last smile as they drove off.

They stood at the gate and waved goodbye to him when Jennifer drove up. She quickly got out of the car and looked at where they were waving to.

"Is James gone? Did I miss him?" She ran up to them.

"Yes dear, he just left. Was there something you needed to say to him?" Sondra was concerned by the look on her face.

It was the way she paced back and forth in front of them that gave Sondra the clue that something wasn't right with Jennifer.

"What is it Jennifer? Are you okay?"

"I'm pregnant!" she blurted out.

Chapter Eight

Sondra stared blankly at her sister. She looked over at Jason and caught a glimpse of his first reaction to her unexpected news. He had closed his eyes and he groaned silently. He took a deep breath and took control of the situation.

He went over to Jennifer who was still pacing and gently pulled her towards him and put his arm around her. She tried to struggle out of his grasp but he held on to her tightly. She felt strength in his arms and for the first time in weeks she felt safe. She burst into uncontrollable tears as he comforted her.

Sondra gulped and watched her husband comfort her baby sister. She felt helpless to do anything. The shock took her completely by surprise.

"Dear God, what do we do now?" she spoke out loud.

Jennifer heard her and she abruptly turned from Jason and confronted Sondra. Anger and confusion took control of her.

"What do you mean 'what do we do?'" she confronted her sister. "It is my problem and I will decide what to do. I'm sick and tired of you and Cassie running my life and telling me what to do. Why don't you both just leave me alone? You have no idea what I am going through," she yelled and went to get back into her car.

"Stop right now, young lady." Jason held her arm to keep her from leaving. "First, you will not speak to my wife in that manner. And second, we are a family and we will work things out as a family. You are not alone in this, Jennifer. We are going inside and we will talk about this." He spoke determinedly and guided her firmly into the house. She went along with him reluctantly.

Sondra looked at her husband and smiled, enjoying his defense of her. She sighed when she thought of what lay ahead of them with Jennifer. She was becoming pensive and uncontrollable. She sighed, thinking that she was just like her at that age. Life was forever and making your own way in life was exciting and challenging. But now there was another life to consider.

When Jennifer sat down in the living room, she put her head on the sofa's plush back. The cream colored soft silk loveseat and sofa was over stuffed with luxurious over stuffed pillows. As she sank into its folds, her heart sank with it. A hard look entered her eyes. When she looked at Jason, she pursed her lips together and said,

"So I wonder what God has in store for me now?" Hoping that he would have the answers, she stared at him with wide eyes.

Jason looked away, unable to comprehend what his part in her life should be. He felt responsible for his brother's action, since he was here at his invitation. He was ready to murder James for putting him in this position. He was hoping to start his own family with his new bride, when all of a sudden he was faced with this complex situation. He closed his eyes and said a quick prayer. Before he could speak, Sondra piped in.

"God makes life, Jennifer, and I know that He has a great plan for you and your baby."

Jason watched his wife gently guide her sister into reality.

"What is it that you want to do about the situation? Have you thought about it at all or are you like us in shock as to what is happening?"

"I don't know what I want to do." Her eyes held tears that came spilling down her face.

Sondra got up from her seat and put her arms around Jennifer and held her tightly.

"We are here for you no matter what decision you make. God will guide you and tell you what you should do, sweetheart. Have some faith in His great plan."

When Jennifer heard God mentioned she pushed her away angrily.

"God is the one who put me in this position. I haven't done anything wrong and now He is punishing me." She got up and went to go out the door.

Jason got up and stopped her from leaving.

"Sit back down, Jennifer. You can't leave until you settle down. Let me get you something to drink and then we can talk some more."

"I am finished talking. I want to go back to school. Gayle is waiting for me. I need to get back to my life and then I will decide if I want to keep this baby or not." Her words came out in angry tones.

Both Jason and Sondra paled at the thought of Jennifer doing the unthinkable by having an abortion.

"Let's calm down and take a breather. Jennifer, why don't you go home and think on this overnight. Sometimes it helps to sleep on things before you make any rash decisions." Jason spoke carefully, trying to calm her down.

"No Jason, I am going back to school right now. My bags are in the car and I need time to think, away from all of you. Please don't be upset with me but I have to do this." She left the house.

Sondra and Jason stared at her as she left the house. Jason sat back down and took his wife's hand.

"We need to start interceding for Jennifer. We have to trust God that she will make the wise decision." He paused as Sondra began to cry. He held her close and prayed.

~

Life went on as usual at the Willow Oaks Ranch. Weeks went by and Sondra and Jason worked the ranch with the ranch hands and came home each night exhausted, not only physically but mentally as well.

Sondra's nerves were shot. She worried about her baby sister and prayed that she would call or answer her phone. It seemed as if she had blocked them out of her life. Sondra prayed that the anger would dissipate and she would come to her senses.

Sondra woke up one morning with a terrible flu. Jason held her head as she vomited in the toilet. Sondra realized that only a special husband would do that for his wife and she was very grateful. Jason called Doctor Martin and he said he would be there that afternoon. When he arrived, Sondra was feeling much better and apologized for disturbing him.

Charles just smiled and took some blood.

"I'm going to run a few tests, Sondra. I'm sure everything will be just fine. I'll let you know what I find out. Meanwhile, why don't you take it easy today? I know how hard you work and being out on the range today probably wouldn't be a good idea." He looked at her seriously.

"How is Jennifer? I haven't heard from her for a couple of weeks and I was concerned for her. She has missed her appointments with her counselor."

Sondra sighed quietly. "She went off to school the day she found out about her pregnancy and we haven't heard from her since. She is not answering our calls and sometimes I fear for the worst. But we are praying."

He shook his head sadly and asked if there was anything he could do.

"But, on a different note, I would like to see you and Jason this afternoon before five o'clock. I will have my nurse set up the appointment."

Sondra wondered why he wanted to see them and started to get worried that something was wrong. She called Jason on his cell phone. Jason said he would be there an hour before the appointment to pick her up.

When they entered his office, Doctor Martin was there smiling at them.

"Well, I don't know if you two are ready for this but it looks like you are going to add someone to your family." They looked at him blankly. He laughed and said more pointedly, "You're going to have a baby!"

Jason looked at Sondra and the biggest smile came on his face. He jumped up and grabbed her and swung her around.

"We're going to have a baby!" he announced. Sondra laughed outright. The two of them looked each other in the eye and Jason kissed her soundly on the lips. Doctor Martin cleared his throat and Sondra went red in the face. It didn't bother Jason one bit.

"Is it a boy or a girl?" He asked the doctor.

He laughed. "Only God knows at this point. I thought the two of you could use some good news."

Sondra sat down on the chair relieved that the news wasn't life threatening. "I'm going to have a baby? What do I do, Doctor Martin?"

"Why, nothing, Sondra. All you have to do is take it easy for the first few months. You may have some morning sickness but if you eat a few crackers before you get up in the morning it might help, I would like you to start taking some prenatal supplements but, besides that, live life as you normally do. It is very normal what you will be going through. I would like to set up monthly visits to check up on you. Why don't you make your first appointment with Sally, in let's say two weeks' time?"

Sondra took a deep breath and the two of them left the office floating on air.

"Oh Jason, are we really are going to have a baby? I didn't think it would happen this quickly."

Jason looked at his bride and drew her close.

"I have dreamed of this day all my life. I can hardly wait for him or her to enter into our lives. I love you, darling. Thank you for loving me." He kissed her again in the hallway.

They left quietly, the news still resonating in their spirits.

Chapter Nine

Jennifer sat on her bed with her back against the wall staring into space. The small dorm room held two twin size beds and two desks. It left little room for anything else. The walls were painted a dusty rose color and a border of stripes circled the room. Gayle's side was untidy with her bed unmade and clothes thrown over it, compared to Jennifer's neat and cozy domain. A fluffy white down comforter covered her body so that only her head was showing. Her sheets were white to match her comforter and two feathery pillows lined the headboard. Jennifer still stared into the night.

Gayle came into the room and threw herself on her bed.

"Well girl, you should have come with me. You can't sit here all day and night by yourself. You have to get out sometime."

Jennifer just sighed.

"I would be terrible company. Nobody wants to go out with a pregnant girl. I can't drink and I know I would want to. Besides, I look terrible."

Gayle looked at Jennifer sitting sideways on her bed with her straight blonde hair neatly falling off her shoulders. Her gorgeous blue eyes and smooth velvety skin make her look like a Barbie doll. She laughed at her friend.

"You are beautiful and besides no one here knows that you are pregnant. You are so thin that you probably won't start showing until you are eight months along. Women would envy that, Jennifer. You are going to have to decide soon what you are going to do."

"I know. I just can't make up my mind. Tomorrow I will be six week along. I still have time to make that decision. I just don't know." She started crying again.

Gayle got up from her bed and went to sit next to Jennifer.

"It's really not a hard decision. Women have abortions all the time. I had one last year and it was perfectly fine. I wasn't ready to be a mother and besides the father wouldn't even acknowledge that I existed." Jennifer looked up sadly, her brown eyes glazing over with hurt.

"I know lots of other girls who have done the same thing. Having a baby is a big decision — one that lasts a lifetime. Do you want that responsibility in your life right now? Are you seriously ready to be a mother? And James will be gone for at least a year, perhaps even eighteen months. Your baby will be three or four months old or even nine months old before he's out of that place. And, who knows? He may never change. Do you want him as a father for your baby, a man that drugged and raped you? And how will you take care of it?"

If Jennifer had looked closer at her friend, she would have seen the pain and anguish in her face. She was trying to convince Jennifer yet in truth she was trying to convince herself that she had done the right thing. But the only person Jennifer was thinking about was herself. She was still wallowing in her self-pity.

~

Cassie moved around the house doing her daily functions automatically. She prayed continuously for her little sister. She was devastated when she found out that she was pregnant, and went back to school. Every day she would call her but she would not answer the phone. The stress and worry was almost too much to bear.

Tommy was worried about his fiancé, Cassie. She was becoming withdrawn and pensive. They would talk for hours about all kinds of subjects but when Jennifer's name was brought up she fretted. He thought he would have a little chat with Jason about what he thought he should do. He had to go over to Willow Oaks to drop off some papers for him to sign, so he thought he would speak to him then.

On the way over, Tommy marveled at the way Jason had wooed Sondra. She was a wild cat before Jason tamed her. She would fight him tooth and nail every time he made a decision on his own. He would have quit the job of managing the ranch if it hadn't been for Cassie. Sondra's temper flared every time they had a confrontation. Tommy was curious what it was that turned her around. He would have to ask Jason what his secret was.

He pulled into the drive way only to find Sondra going out to the barn. She stopped and waited for him to get out of the car.

"Hello, Tommy. What brings you to Willow Oaks this fine day? And, by the way, you are doing such a wonderful job managing the ranch hands at Parker Valley. Thank you for that. I'm sorry that I haven't thanked you enough for all you do for us but I would like to rectify that. I really appreciate you, Tommy." She gave him a big smile.

She had a certain glow about her today that Tommy couldn't put his finger on. He again marveled at the change in her attitude towards him.

"Why Sondra, thank you for that compliment and it is a pleasure to work with you. You have managed the ranch so well that it was very simple to walk in your footsteps. You look especially wonderful today."

"Why thank you, Tommy. Are you looking for Jason? He is in the house going over some figures in the office. Why don't you go right in?" She continued to walk to the barn.

The barn was almost bigger than the house. They could house at least twenty to thirty horses, and the stable manager Kenneth lived in a little apartment above the barn. It was a cozy little place with a full kitchen, two bedrooms and a lovely living room. He lived there with his lovely wife Janet who shared a lot of the duties with her husband. They were an elderly couple who were unable to have children but were grandparents to all the children that lived on the ranch and those of the ranch hands who lived in town. They loved their job and they treated their horses just like they would their children.

Jason held family events that encompassed all the ranches in the district. Everyone looked forward to them in the late fall. They were planning one such event next month and everyone was starting to make comments on how they were looking forward to it. It was the beginning of October and the pumpkins were just beginning to be big enough to pick for their fall decorations. The children would go on hayrides throughout the range and have competitions with bull riding and barrel races. It was a great time for all the families to get together. Sondra still marveled at her husband's ability to bring people together.

She passed a small bench just inside the barn and remembered her first encounter with her husband, Jason. He had never been that angry with her as he was that day. Those were the days not long ago when she was rebellious and stubborn, and it took all of Jason's patience to cultivate Sondra into trusting him and captivating her heart. She sighed and realized how much she loved him. She put her hand on her stomach and thanked God that she was actually going to have his baby. Secretly, she hoped it was a boy. She could imagine another Jason running around. How proud she would be to see him grow up like his daddy.

It was then that she remembered Jennifer and wondered how she was and what she was thinking. She still couldn't believe that the two of them were having a baby at the same time. She was unable to tell her the good news. If only she would allow them into her life again. She had gone through a great loss-with the death of their parents-and now her body was going through these changes. They could help each other through the ups and downs of pregnancy, if only she could reach inside her soul and comfort her and reason with her. She sighed again and said a small prayer for her little sister.

~

Cassie was also praying for Jennifer. She would spend each morning taking at least an hour of quiet time and pray for the upcoming day and now especially for her little Jennifer. She cried silently, praying God would penetrate the stubborn exterior of her heart. She had changed in the last year from a quiet, gentle child to a feisty stubborn woman. Rebellion was always a way to destruction. This whole problem stemmed from her going against Jason's request that she and James have nothing to do with each other. But we all have choices to make and we must live with the consequences of those choices.

She had prayed for hours on end for Sondra too. She was stubborn and independent also but God had changed her heart just like she believed He would do for Jennifer. The harder she prayed, the stronger her faith became. She would lay her worries at the cross and give them to Jesus to carry. It was too heavy for her.

~

Tommy entered the house and called out for Jason. He went into the office and found him nestled amongst a stack of paperwork.

"Why don't you let me handle some of that work for you Jason? he queried. "It's the least I can do for all you have done for me."

"Hello, Tommy. There would be nothing I would like better to do than hand this over to you but it involves some legal documents that I have to go through. It won't take me much longer." He got up from his desk and went around greeting him with a handshake.

"What can I do for you, brother?"

"I came to drop these off for you to sign but I would like to spend a few minutes talking to you about Cassie if I may. I hate to take you away from your work but I am really concerned about her."

"No problem. I have a little bit of time to spend with you. Please sit down." He motioned for him to sit on the brown leather love seat. He took the leather chair opposite him. "What seems to be the problem?"

"Well, to tell you the truth, I think our whole problem stems from her interfering and trying to control her sisters. Jennifer is a prime example. She is always mollycoddling and pampering her. I think that is one reason that she went out with James to begin with. I heard them arguing with each other and Jennifer telling her to 'stay out of her personal life and that she would do as she pleased'. I wanted to step in at that moment and calm the situation down but I felt that I shouldn't interfere. Now, I wonder if I should have. Cassie means well but she can be very demanding and controlling. She is a perfectionist in every sense of the word and expects everyone to be the same way. I am having difficulty adjusting to her constant controlling behavior. I realize that she has gifts and talents that I don't have but she won't allow me to be the man in our relationship. Sometimes I would like to strangle her but she is difficult to talk to. I'm at my wits end and sometimes feel like giving up." He hung his head in his hand ashamed of his behavior.

Jason sat there and listened quietly taking in all that Tommy had to say. He wanted to help his friend but he wanted to be sure that he gave the right advice.

"I know how you feel, brother, but sometimes the only thing we can do is go to the Lord and ask for His divine intervention. It was the same with Sondra and me. There were times when I was so angry and frustrated with her behavior that I hate to admit it but I lost my control. The last thing you want to do is resort to anger. Besides, we want our women to be feisty and independent. They make for better wives. You wouldn't want someone who didn't have a mind of their own. Our women need to be nurtured and treasured and honored. Bringing out the best in them requires patience on our part."

"And it requires a lot of prayer," Tommy answered back with a smile on his face.

"Prayer is the utmost. I spent hours on my knees for Sondra. When I showed her the love and respect she deserved, but with a firm hand, she came around and began to see me differently. No matter what she did to me, it was forgiven and talked about. One of the keys to our relationship is communication. I insist that we talk about all our differences immediately before they get out of hand. Most of the problems we have had are through misunderstandings. The only way to handle it is talk it out and make sure the right information is given. That goes for my part too. I'm not always the most reasonable person to get along with and I'm not always right. In fact, most of the time, it's better to be reconciled than to be right."

"I see what you mean. But Cassie won't listen to me when it comes to her sisters. They have become the most important thing to her. How do I turn that around and make it so that I am the most important thing in her life?"

"Communication, buddy. That is still the key. You have to tell her how you are feeling and how she makes you feel. If she doesn't know, she can't do anything about it. If she won't talk to you, make it an ultimatum. That will make her listen and make sure that you are firm about talking straight. Don't pull any punches. She needs to hear the truth from you, Tommy. Both of you are special and I believe you are soul mates. You need to take the high road. Let her know that you are serious and will not take no for an answer but do it in a way that is respectful. I guarantee that she will come around and understand your feelings. She needs a lot of under-standing now especially with the way Jennifer is acting. There are times that I would like to take that young lady in hand but it is not up to me. Someone will come along and be her strength. I only hope that it is soon," he said.

"I agree. Thank you, Jason, for listening to me and I hope and pray along with you that Jennifer will come around." He smiled and got up to leave.

"Before you go, let me pray for you," he said. He put his hand on his shoulder and began to pray.

"Father, we come before you endeavoring to be humble men of God. We love you, Lord, and ask that you give us strength and comfort in our times of need. Tommy has come with a broken heart and a wounded spirit. Lord, please comfort him and give him wisdom when it comes to the love of his life. Change his heart to be like yours Father and give them both the courage to be submissive before you. Father, I ask that you give Tommy and Cassie the gift of communication. It is the essence of who you are, Lord. You gave us your Word so that we could be instructed and you gave us Jesus to be our example and so that we could communicate with you. Help us first to honor you with our prayers and come before you with our concerns. Instruct us Father in your ways. We ask this in the mighty name of Jesus. Amen." Jason looked up at Tommy and stood up to give him a hug.

"I look forward to hearing what God is going to do in your life, Tommy. And I hope that the two of you set that wedding date before too long."

"Thank you, Jason. I covet your prayers and hope you will continue to pray. Please ask Sondra to do the same." He left quietly, his heart lightened by Jason's words.

Jason sat in his office and continued to pray for Tommy and Cassie. It was never easy when it came to the Parker girls. They were one in a million, and he won the prize.

Chapter Ten

James looked at the calendar that was hanging in his room and realized that he had been in this place for almost three weeks. It felt like three months. He had never done so much soul searching in his whole life than he did in the last three weeks. He felt like his whole life had been wasted with his foolish antics and his spoiled and selfish ways.

He came in with an attitude of coasting until he could get out of here and go back to the way life was before, except he would be more careful. But he discovered that the way of life he was living was just a cover up for deep emotional hang-ups.

Two of his roommates were drug addicts and the other man was full of anger and violence when he drank. At first, James thought it would be hell living with three other men but he soon realized that living in such close proximity bonded them in a way that they became inseparable. They learned each other's quirks and strange habits, realizing that they were all too similar. They learned to get along and support each other in their weaknesses.

Initially, James thought he was better than any of the others because his addiction was not drugs or alcohol but he soon came to realize that his sex addiction was more destructive since it involved innocent women.

When he arrived at the center, he was surprised that it was in the country with the closest neighbor being at least one and a half miles away. It was a large white stucco three story house with seven large bedrooms for the patients that housed twenty men. There were two house parents and three counselors. The head of the house parents was Mary, a registered nurse, and her husband, Bill, was a doctor. He soon came to know that it was their home they were staying in and they were in charge. He liked the kind look in Mary's eyes, but was wary of Bill's commanding inflexible ways. It reminded him of his brother Jason, and he was immediately defensive. It only took two days for him to change his mind and respect him when he watched him deal with the problems of his fellow houseguests.

The first week felt like an orientation week. He was instructed on the do's and don'ts of the house rules. He learned that he could not have communication with the outside world for at least a month and, afterwards, that would be up to the discretion of the house parents. The only contact he could have would be in an emergency. He also learned that he was not bound to the home but could leave at any time, usually forfeiting all your tuition. And, in James's case, he could possibly face criminal charges if he didn't complete the program and if Jennifer pressed charges. They were comfortable that you would stay at least until they could convince you otherwise. They were very strict with their program.

It was grueling at first, getting up at the crack of dawn for devotionals and singing, and then on to group therapy followed up by individual counseling. It was a working ranch and after their sessions they all had chores to do. James was used to working on Jason's ranch so the work duty was not an issue for him.

James was curious and he watched and studied the other men that had been there for a long period of time and how they had come through their addictions. One man had been there on a court order. If he didn't succeed, he would be sent to four years in prison for drug possession. He was a big burly young man of only twenty five years. His hardened look stemmed from years of drug use.

James learned that he had been sexually molested at age five and every year until he was fourteen. He moved out of his house at age fourteen and lived on the street for four years, making his money from prostitution and selling drugs. He found out later that Andy had stumbled on a group of Christian men who went out in the street to minister to the street kids. He was intrigued by them and began following them and listening to their teachings. They would spend hours talking to him and urging him to get off the street. They would find him a place to stay. One day Andy made the mistake of selling his drugs to a special drug enforcement agent and was caught and taken to jail. When the group had found out what had happened to him they pleaded with the judge to let him go to a Teen Challenge Center. They would pay for him to go there. The judge took pity on the young man and gave him an ultimatum of going there, or four years in prison. Andy was grateful for the reprieve and has been there ever since. He was one of the special counselors.

When James listened to the life stories of some of the men, he couldn't help but feel blessed that he had the upbringing that he had. He hadn't been abused or molested or abandoned. He felt ashamed of the way he had taken his life for granted. He had grown up in a life of privilege and was loved by his parents and siblings. He kept asking himself why had he gone down the road he was traveling?

Doctor Bill already understood why James had been acting the way he did. He had seen it hundreds of times. Fear, jealousy and inadequacy were the roots behind his behavior. Their job was to determine when it began and put an end to it. Individual counseling would be the key to their success if he was willing to be vulnerable.

They prayed especially hard for him during his counseling sessions after they had received the call that his victim, his sister-in-law was pregnant. They also knew after a few days talking in sessions that he could possibly be in love with her. Mary was convinced that he was a special young man who could be turned around quickly. He showed much promise when he broke down and confessed everything he had done. His addiction was strong and they were determined to root out the cause.

His love of the Lord was another key to his success. He had been brought up with a strong Christian background but his rebellion turned him away from God. They pinpointed that his rebellion began with pressure to succeed like his brother Jason. He had been the perfect son, and in James's mind he could never live up to him. Everything his brother touched turned to gold. How could he possibly compete with that? Their job was to reprogram James to believe that he was God's special son and He had a different plan for his life. He was to come out of the shadow of his brother and become the man that God created him to be.

Mary learned from her sessions with him that he had a special gift of communication. His gift of the English language was one that could take him right to the pulpit. When he spoke, he spoke with conviction and honesty and he could convince you of anything. He could capti-vate the room with just a simple sentence. Mary noticed how the others were drawn to him and listened to him. His sandy blonde hair and deep blue eyes could melt your soul. His charismatic personality and good looks charmed everyone. She believed that his calling would be to preach the Word of God.

Mary had a dream one night that millions would come to the Lord through his gifting's. She became very excited when she shared it in the middle of the night with her husband.

"It was so real, Bill!" she exclaimed when she woke him up to tell him of her dream. "I saw millions bow their knees to Jesus and James was the mediator."

"That's wonderful, Mary. Now go back to sleep." He was too sleepy to listen to her.

Mary couldn't sleep after her dream, so she got up and immediately went into prayer for James. She couldn't get it out of her spirit. She truly believed that this was his calling. She had to be careful not to tell him but allow God to work in his spirit and bring it forth through revelation. She felt giddy with excitement.

"Thank you, Jesus?" She felt like shouting at the top of her lungs.

~

James had a dream that night too. He dreamt of Jennifer writhing in pain. She was on a gurney with a white sheet draped over her. Blood covered the white sheet and she sat up and started screaming for him. The frightened look on her face as she stared at him with tears, mixed with mascara running down her cheeks, made her look very frightening.

He woke with a startled grunt and sat up on his bed and looked around, expecting to see her. His dream was so real. He shook his head to try and eliminate the picture in his mind.

"Dear God, please take care of Jennifer," he muttered, fear taking control of him as he started to shake.

"Are you okay, buddy?" his roommate Jonathan whispered to him from the top bunk.

"I don't know. I just had the most horrible dream," he said. He was still shaking.

"Do you want to talk about it?" Jonathan sat up in bed looking at James with a smile. "Sometimes it helps to talk about our demons."

He looked at his friend and said shook his head yes. They had bonded over the past three weeks and James felt like he could be trusted with his innermost thoughts.

The two of them went out of the room and tiptoed into the kitchen, trying not to wake anyone up.

Jonathan went into the fridge and poured himself a glass of milk.

"Would you like some?"

"No thanks," James replied. He sat down on the kitchen stool and put his head in his hands. "I can't shake this feeling I get inside."

"Tell me about it!"

"There is this girl I know that I wasn't very kind too. She is now my sister-in-law and I took advantage of her. I think I was so jealous of my brother marrying someone who he was so in love with and I didn't have anyone. I've tried to compare myself to him constantly and I never seem to measure up. I'm so ashamed to admit that I hurt her. When she left my bed there was blood on the sheets. I had no idea that she was a virgin. I felt terrible. I have never made love to a virgin before. All the women I dated were very sexually active. I think I was drawn to her sweet innocence. She is a very special girl and I took away from her what was most sacred."

Just talking about it made James cry. His cry came in great gulps deep down inside his soul.

Jonathan put his arm around him trying to console his friend.

"Get it all out, James," he said gently.

After he settled down somewhat he spoke again.

"The dream I had was her lying on a gurney with blood all over a white sheet. I thought of her innocence that had been taken from her. She was crying out to me. I don't know what to do! What if she is hurt? God, forgive me. I didn't mean to hurt her." He cried again with his face in his hands.

The two of them spoke for long hours into the night, praying and seeking forgiveness from God. It was a time that was full of great healing for both of them. Jonathan also shared his deepest fears with James and the two of them laid it all at the foot of the cross and felt the spirit of forgiveness washing over them.

Mary sat at the bottom of the stairs listening to them talk and prayed that God would use this time to heal their broken hearts. She felt that her prayers had been answered and whispered under her breath, 'God is so good!'

Chapter Eleven

Jennifer lay very still on the table with a white sheet covering her. She took a deep breath as she waited for the nurse to come in. 'What am I doing here?' she asked herself as she studied the flowers on the wall.

Her friend, Gayle, was waiting for her in the waiting room. They had quite a time getting from the car to the clinic. There was a man and woman on the sidewalk outside with pamphlets begging her not to go through with the procedure. She could still envision the face of the woman with gray hair and kind blue eyes, who looked at her with love in her eyes and told her that she was going to be alright, and that God loved her as she entered the building.

She was so unnerved by the experience that she walked into the clinic in a stupor. She was greeted by an official looking nurse who was a no nonsense woman in her late forties. She was told to take a seat and was given long documents to sign. Jennifer was so nervous that she couldn't read everything she was signing, so she just signed where it was marked X. She just wanted to get the procedure over with.

She had made the decision the night before and she and Gayle made plans to have it done the next day, before she could change her mind. Gayle insisted that she drive her to the clinic and they left first thing in the morning. She must have been the first patient that day, as there was no one else in the waiting room.

The nurse eventually ushered her into a little room and told her to take off all of her clothes and lie down on the table. She was given a white sheet to put over her.

Jennifer nervously removed her clothing and folded them neatly and set them on the chair beside the table. She stood there naked and tried to remind herself why she was there again. She climbed up on the cold table with white paper lining it. When she looked around the room she noticed very strange stainless steel equipment, and wondered what its use was.

All around her, soft spa-like music was playing which eased her spirit a little. She felt like she was there for a facial except for the absence of the warm blankets and towels, and the smell of incense. Instead she was covered by a cold white sheet and it smelled like a hospital.

As she lay on the table, all kinds of thoughts ran through her mind, but she couldn't get the face of that lovely lady with the gray hair out of her mind. She said that God loved her. 'Did He really love her?' If He did, she wouldn't be in this terrible position of lying on a cold hard table about to get rid of the baby that was growing inside of her.

Jennifer started to shake visibly. She couldn't stop the shaking. 'Dear God, please tell me again what am I doing here?'she thought to herself. She couldn't think clearly. Gayle had given her something that morning to calm her nerves. 'It must be muddling up my mind,' she thought quietly. She tried to concentrate on the yellow flowers on the wall. She tried counting them, but she still couldn't stop the shaking.

It was at that moment that the doctor came in.

"Hello, Miss Parker, is it?" he inquired. She shook her head yes.

"I understand that you are here willingly to take care of the little problem you have growing inside you?" Casually he looked down at her chart. "You are not allergic to anything I assume?" He looked up at her, waiting for her response.

"No sir, not that I am aware of. I have never had an operation before so I don't know." Her words sounded a little slurred to her. She noticed that he was a young doctor probably just out of med school. He couldn't be any more than twenty-one years old. She wanted to ask him where his credentials were but couldn't get the words out.

"That's good," he mumbled. The nurse came in and he said to her casually, "Let's get started." He moved closer to her and began to take down the equipment he was going to use.

"Have you had anything to eat or drink this morning, Miss Parker?" He asked while he took a large needle and filled it with some fluid and was getting ready to inject her.

"My roommate gave me something to calm my nerves. I don't know what it was." She answered as steadily as she could under the circumstances. She still couldn't stop her shaking.

The doctor muttered something to the nurse and she left the room. He busied himself with the equipment and looked at the nurse with a question when she came back in.

"It was just a minor sedative, doctor," she told him in a businesslike fashion.

"Thank you, nurse. Could you please prep the patient?"

The nurse told Jennifer to move her bottom down to the end of the table and put her feet in the stirrups that she brought out from the side of the table. The metal was cold on her feet which didn't help her shaking. She gulped in anticipation of what was going to happen. Before she could ask, the doctor started to explain the procedure. She could hardly understand the words he was using but she pretended to know what he was talking about.

She couldn't see what he was doing so she just started to pray that it would end soon. If only she could stop her shaking. Just as he was about to insert a sharp needle, the room went pitch black.

"I can't believe this is happening," the doctor said to the nurse. He put the needle down and told Jennifer to slide back up on the bed. He ordered her to wait there and he would be back as soon as he could figure out what the problem was.

Jennifer put her head down on the small pillow that was there and kept still. The door opened and closed and she wondered who had come into the dark room. A small voice whispered into her ear and told her to 'run.' The person left the room as quietly as they had come in.

Jennifer started shaking again. "Dear God, what am I doing here?" She cried in a panic. "God forgive me for what I was about to do." She jumped off the table and quickly put her clothes back on. She ran out of the room and into the waiting room as fast as she could. She grabbed Gayle and told her she was leaving.

"But wait! Did you have the procedure?" she asked her friend as they rushed out of the clinic.

Jennifer kept running as the woman in the room told her to do. She looked back at the clinic and saw a strange woman in the window smiling at her. The next second she vanished. Jennifer blinked and suddenly realized that she must have been an angel. She had been waiting for a sign for three weeks and finally God answered her. She was to keep her baby. She laughed and cried all at once.

"Did you see that, Gayle?" She grabbed her friend and looked into her eyes.

"See what?" she asked. She looked at Jennifer as if she was crazy.

"There was an angel in the window." She giggled and began to dance around on the sidewalk.

She looked over to the right and the woman with the gray hair smiled at her and waved. 'Was that another angel?'

"God, you are too wonderful. Gayle, God wants me have this baby. There is a life growing inside of me and I want to see him or her grow up to be big and strong. Perhaps they might grow up to be the president of the United States. Anything he or she wants to be. I will see to it that they reach whatever goals they desire. I'm free to make that choice, Gayle, and I choose life for my baby." She danced around again happily. "Thank you, God," she repeated over and over.

Gayle looked at her as if she had lost her mind. But she joined in the celebration. At least she made her choice. That was all that mattered.

As they headed back to the dorm room, Jennifer asked her about the power failure.

"There was no power failure, at least not that I was aware of," she said.

"Are you serious? It only happened in my room?" She laughed again. "It was a miracle I tell you, Gayle. God showed me a miracle. I was praying all night for a sign and He gave me one. I am so happy and so blessed."

Gayle just sighed and said she was glad it was Jennifer having the baby and not her.

The two of them went out for breakfast. Jennifer was starving.

Chapter Twelve

Cassie busied herself with her daily chores that morning with a renewed vengeance. She believed, if she kept herself busy, the days would go faster and she wouldn't have to think about her problems. She always believed that if you focus on others your problems seem lighter. She was hand cleaning the stove with her gloves and an oven cleaner when the call came in. She was tempted to let it ring and let the answering machine get it but today it sounded too insistent.

She picked up the phone on the fourth ring.

"Hello?"

"Oh Cassie, I'm so sorry. Can you ever forgive me?" A voice that sounded so distant came through weakly.

"Jennifer, sweetheart is that you? Oh honey, are you okay?" She started to cry. She was so grateful to finally hear her voice after three weeks of silence.

Jennifer started crying on the phone too. Cassie just let her sob. She gently tried to soothe her by saying 'it's okay, darling.' The two of them sobbed together.

Finally, Jennifer was cried out and they actually were able to talk to each other.

"Are you okay, sweetheart? Can you tell me what has been going on?"

"Oh Cassie, I just want to come home. Can I come home? Will you hate me?" She started sobbing again.

"Oh course you can come home. This is your home as much as it is mine. You are always welcome here. Come right now. It's not that far. Do you need help packing up your things?" She kept asking practical questions.

"I don't have very much stuff," she sniffled. "Gayle will help me put it in the car. I should be there later this evening. There is so much I have to tell you." She started sobbing again.

When Cassie put down the phone she put her head in her hands and cried.

After a few minutes, she went down on her knees in the kitchen and prayed.

"Thank you, Jesus, for bringing our little Jennifer home. Please take care of her. She needs you so much, Lord. Bring her home safely," she cried out happily.

Tommy heard her crying in the kitchen and came in from the office.

"Are you okay, honey?" He was almost afraid to ask. Lately, she would cry at the least little thing. She pushed him away at every turn of event. He wanted to make sure it wasn't serious this time.

"Oh Tommy, it was Jennifer on the phone. She is coming home! Can you believe it? She is actually coming home! I am so grateful to God, Tommy. I'm sorry I have been such a cry baby. My nerves are shot. How do you ever put up with me?" She cried in his arms as he held her.

"I'm glad things worked out, sweetheart. I knew she would come home. She is a very sensible girl. She has good genes in her."

He stroked her hair with a loving gesture. Just feeling her in his arms made his heart ache. They have been so distant lately and Tommy had missed her gentle cuddling and kisses. He bent down and kissed her gently on the lips. She responded in kind with an ardent kiss of her own. Before it could get too passionate, Tommy picked her up and carried her into the living room and set her down on the couch. He stood in front of her and folded his arms across his chest and confronted her.

"I think it is time that you and I had a little talk, sweetheart." Sternness came into his voice.

"I have missed you greatly over the last few weeks and I think we should get some things settled before too much time passes."

Cassie took a big gulp and knew what was coming. She deserved to be chastised for the way she had been acting. Each night, she went to bed asking God forgiveness for her behavior when she knew she should also be asking Tommy's.

She bent her head in shame and Tommy put his hand under her chin and looked her in the eyes.

"I love you, Cassie. I care about you and what you are going through. If we can't share our hurts our sorrows and our fears, where does that leave us? It leaves us empty and alone. I won't have that in my relationship with you. It is all or nothing with me. Either we are together or not. You have shut me out of your life for the last time." He paced back and forth. He stopped and looked at her seriously.

"I am going to be your husband — to love, cherish and honor you for the rest of your life. I expect nothing less from you. You have not honored me as someone you want to share your life with. You have closed off a part of you that I want to hold and comfort, and more importantly you have shut God out of our relationship. You must make a decision whether you want me to be part of your life or not. Will you consider that, Cassie? I'm in this for a lifetime and I won't put up with what you have been doing to me. Do you understand?" He spoke firmly but kindly.

Cassie looked back at him with tearful eyes.

"I have been selfish and terribly rude to you, Tommy, and I am very sorry. I hope you will forgive me for my behavior." She took a deep breath. "I won't make excuses for myself. I have been a shrew to you and I have shut you out. I am not used to leaning on anyone and I am sorry that you felt left out of my life. I can't promise I won't do it again but I will try my best to honor you in the future. Will you forgive me?" She looked into his eyes.

"Of course I will forgive you, sweetheart. That is what we do for one another. But next time you try to shut me out you and I will have it out! Is that clear? I want to know how you tick, what makes you sad, and what makes you happy. I love your laugh and believe it or not I love your tears. Both give me pleasure to be a part of your life because that is what life is all about. Laughter and tears make up 'who' we are, Cassie, and we share both in good times and in bad. I'm not just here for the ride. I'm here for the long haul. Okay?" He bent down and pulled her into his arms.

He whispered in her ear. "I also think we should make a date for our wedding. I want to be your husband, Cassie Parker." He kissed her firmly on the lips.

Cassie fell into his arms and wept. He held her and stroked her hair. The two of them held on to each other for at least an hour and shared their hearts for the first time since Jason and Sondra were married. They finally came up with a date for their wedding.

~

Sondra received the call just before lunch. When she got off the phone she jumped up and down and praised the Lord.

"Jason!" she shouted running throughout the house. "She's coming home!"

Jason came out of the office and wondered what all the commotion was about. He worried that something had happened to Sondra.

110

She flew into his arms and happily put her arms around his neck and gave him a long lasting kiss.

"Well, my dear. I'll take that any day of the week. And may I ask what has made you so excited?"

"Oh Jason, Jennifer is coming home. Cassie just called and told me she had a talk with her. She sounded so excited about it. I just pray that everything is okay with her." She thought suddenly that things may not be quite the way they were expecting.

"Jason, what if she had an abortion? I can't even imagine her going through that all alone. Cassie said she kept asking her forgiveness for the way she acted. Oh my God, Jason, what if it's true? How will we handle it?"

Jason pulled her close again and kissed her forehead.

"When will you ever learn to have faith in your sister? She is from good stock. I'm sure that she did whatever she felt she needed to do. We must trust God with this, Sondra, and support anything that she has decided to do. Okay? Will you trust the Lord in this?"

Sondra put her head on his chest and sighed. "I do trust God, Jason. I pray that Jennifer will do the same thing. He has such a great plan for our lives. We have to convince her of that."

Jason marveled at how far his precious wife had come in trusting in God and trusting his advice. At that moment, he couldn't have loved her any more than he did right now. He picked her up and carried her upstairs to their bedroom.

Chapter Thirteen

Sondra and Jason, along with Claira, had dinner over at the Parker Valley Ranch that night hoping to greet Jennifer when she got home. They were all pensive, wondering what news she would have to give them. They prayed silently that she was well and had made good decisions.

When she walked through the door, it was like a family reunion. Tears of joy were mixed with hugs and kisses. They all waited patiently for her to tell them of the news of the fate of her baby. Finally, she confronted them all and told them of her experience at the clinic. Sondra held her breath as Jennifer told the story, wondering about the outcome. When she explained how God had sent her an angel to tell her to run, they all breathed a sigh of relief.

"Oh my goodness, Jennifer, it must have been a terrible thing for you to have to go through alone," Claira said. She hugged her precious sister.

"It had to have been an angel. We were certainly praying for you, Jennifer. The heavens must have been wondering where all those prayers for you were coming from. It is so exciting to know how God listens to us. I am so overwhelmed." Cassie started to cry. "This little one you are carrying must have an amazing job to do for the Lord."

Sondra listened to her baby sister talk about her experiences. Finally, when things started to calm down, she took her aside and told her the good news they had to share.

"We are going to have a baby too, Jennifer. I think we might have gotten pregnant around the same time. Can you imagine it?" she laughed. They gave each other hugs.

"Sondra, what wonderful news! You must be so excited about it. Just imagine you and me going through the same thing at the same time. God really is good, isn't He?" She started to cry.

"Truthfully, Sondra, I was so confused about what I was going to do. I was angry about being pregnant. I thought God had left me. I should have stayed here and worked it out with the help of my family. Can you ever forgive me for treating you so badly? I feel like I grew up in those weeks. I was depressed and unforgiving. I'm surprised God would have anything to do with me because of my rebellion. I'm so ashamed." She put her head in her hands and sobbed.

Sondra wrapped her arms around her and the two of them cried together.

"It's okay, sweetie. We all have gone through similar things in our life, especially with mom and dad's death. I still can't believe they are gone." She looked at Jennifer and smiled. "They would have been so proud of you, honey, just as I am."

~

For the next few months, Sondra and Jennifer tried the patience of all those around them, running around trying to satisfy their food cravings and putting up with their moods and tantrums and what Jason found the worst were the fits of uncontrollable crying.

Sondra didn't suffer from morning sickness but Jennifer did. Everywhere she went she had to take a bag with her.

When their bodies started changing, new clothes had to be purchased. Claira decided to start a new line of maternity clothes for her shop. She called the new line 'Claira & Me.' It took off with all her customers far and wide, especially her clients in the Country and Western Celebrity Gang. She actually had specially designed a new 'Claira & Me' wardrobe for Lynn Callahan, the up and coming country superstar who was expecting her first child. Her husband Tony told Claira to make her look 'Mommy Sexy.' That is just what she did. Now her line was selling all over the country thanks to the different social media outlets and the new web site. Sondra's and Jennifer's pregnancies were a business blessing to Claira.

She had her clothes manufactured by a company in Dallas. Her garments were individually designed to fit certain clients so she needed an experienced group to execute her creations and hired a handful of creative women who designed the new concepts in the back of her store.

She built a room behind the shop that held cutting tables for her pattern maker. It was an exciting venture and proved to be very successful — especially with the backing of Jason's financial means. He was thirty percent owner of Claira's Designs and proved to be a wonderful business partner. In fact, the shop was so successful they wondered how long it would be before they were able to look at more inexpensive labor markets to manufacture their designs.

~

Sondra sauntered in the office dressed in her new riding clothes that gave her a little more room in her stomach.

"Good morning, darling. Is there anything you need before I take off on Sasha? I thought I would ride out with the hands and check up on our cattle and see how they are progressing." She smiled confidently.

"No, sweetheart. Are you sure you will be alright? Do you need any help?" He stood up behind his desk and gave her a smile. "If not, I'm just going to finish up on the Johnson Deal. We should be ready to take over in the next few weeks so I will have to be out of town. I hate leaving you alone," he replied. He braced himself and expecting her to burst into a tantrum.

"No, I'm going to be just fine. Jennifer and I will go into the city for our ultra sounds. I was hoping you could go too, to see our little baby. But if you can't, I understand."

He shook his head. "I can postpone my meeting. When is your appointment?"

"Our appointment is on Friday afternoon. We thought we would make a day out of it and go for lunch and do some shopping. We would love to have you come along. Thank you Jason." She danced out of the room before he could back out of it.

Jason groaned, not relishing the thought of going shopping with the girls. Perhaps he could arrange an appointment and meet the girls at the clinic. He would do just that he thought happily. Just then the phone rang and he answered it quickly.

"Jason Nelson, can I help you?"

There was silence on the other end of the phone. "Hello?" he said again. Then the line went dead. He looked at the caller ID and it said out of area with no number to call back. "That is strange," he thought to himself. The phone rang again and he picked it up curiously.

"Yes, what can I help you with?" His voice became louder to the caller.

"If you know what is good for you, you will stop the Johnson Project. That's if you value your sister-in-law, Jennifer. I hear she will be having a baby. Drop the case and nothing will happen to her," threatened a muffled voice disguised so that he couldn't recognize it.

"Who is this? If you lay one hand on Jennifer I will hunt you down myself. Do you understand me?" He heard the phone click.

Jason stood there with the phone in his hand as anger and fear rose to the surface. He immediately called the operator and asked if they could trace the call that just came in. When she said that she couldn't, he hung up and called the police. His anger continued to consume him when the police arrived to question him.

At the end of the questioning, Jason felt that the police couldn't do anything unless a crime had been committed. He was afraid that just a menacing call wouldn't qualify as a crime. He paced back and forth wondering what to do about the call and decided to take matters in his own hands.

His first thought was to call in one of his best friends and lead ranch hand, Andrew Walker. He came from Virginia with Jason and had been with him ever since he started the ranch almost a year ago. They were room-mates at Harvard and quickly became friends. They were from similar backgrounds. After graduation, Jason went one way and Andrew went into the Navy. After four years, he was eventually asked to join the Navy Seals. They kept in close contact during the last ten years and, when Andrew left the Navy, Jason invited him to the ranch as his body guard. He went undercover as a ranch hand. Jason had received death threats before and took every precaution he could to keep him and his family safe. Andrew stayed on to help his friend. His Navy Seal days were over but his expertise always came in handy.

You didn't reach where Jason was today without stepping on a few toes. He did everything by the book but, in most deals, there are winners and losers and sometimes the losers got angry. Andrew was a blessing to have around.

When Jason felt it was no longer necessary to have protection, he gave him the option of staying and taking on the responsibility of running the ranch hands. Andrew loved the outdoors and soon cattle ranching was in his blood. He rode a horse better than anyone he knew. But Jason still relied on his strong character as his biggest asset.

He trusted Andrew with his life. He was single, young, and made a good looking cowboy, with dark hair and clear grayish green eyes. He was of medium build but was strong as an ox. He was a no nonsense man who ran his team with a firm hand. The ranch hands respected him and worked hard for him as well as for their keep.

When he came into the office, he stood tall and greeted Jason with a nod.

"Andrew, my friend, I want to thank you for taking time to come in and see me." He stood up and shook his hand. "I know how busy you are but we have a bit of a problem." He motioned for him to sit on the leather couch. Jason sat opposite him. Andrew frowned when he saw the serious look on Jason's face.

"What is it, Jason?" he asked.

"I just got a threatening call. I have no idea who it was from but they told me to drop the Johnson Project or they would hurt my sister-in-law Jennifer." He shifted in his chair but Andrew sat up straighter giving Jason his full attention.

"What can I do for you, Jason?" he inquired.

"I know this is going to be different for you, Andrew, but I need you to look after Jennifer. You know that she has been through some hard times and being pregnant doesn't make things easier. She is young, impetuous, hard-headed, and sometimes downright rude but she is a sweet young girl and doesn't deserve to be brought into my messes. I would hate to see anything happen to her. Do you think you could take on that responsibility?"

Andrew took a minute to think about it and shook his head yes.

"I would do anything for you, Jason. We have been friends for a long time. I haven't babysat a girl yet and I'm sure it will be a challenge. Are you going to tell her why I will be shadowing her?" He asked the question without blinking an eye.

"Yes. Otherwise she will rebel and you won't have a prayer following her around." Jason began to chuckle when he saw the look on his friend's face.

Andrew didn't think it was funny and silently groaned, 'Not a spoiled brat, God please!'

"Do I have any parameters to follow? What if she doesn't want me around? Can I force her to do things my way? You know I am pretty strict when it comes to safety," he said.

Jason laughed again. "Just use your common sense, Andrew. I trust you with her. She will have to follow your rules. I will insist on it. We must keep her safe. I didn't like the sound of that call one bit," he added on a serious note. "My family means everything to me."

Chapter Fourteen

"I will not have someone following me day in and day out and that is final. Jason, I can take care of myself." When she saw the look in his eye she added pleadingly, "Please don't make me do this. It was probably just a prank call anyway." Jennifer couldn't shake off her nervous feeling.

"You do not have a say in this. Andrew will not be in your face at all times. He will just be around checking on things and making sure that you are safe. He will sleep upstairs in the guest room and you will follow his instructions. Are you clear on this, Jennifer? Your safety means the entire world to me and I won't take no for an answer. You will do as you are told. Andrew can be forceful at times and I have given him the authority to do what it takes to make you safe, like it or not."

Jennifer's stubborn resistance was really starting to irritate him. He hated doing this to her but her safety was everything to him. If anything ever happened to her, he wouldn't be able to forgive himself.

He was hoping that she would have been more accommodating but, given that she was Sondra's sister, he should have known she wouldn't take it easily. They were both independent and sometimes very difficult to get along with. It took him many painstaking hours of prayer to tame Sondra, and God help Andrew with Jennifer.

At this point, as long as she was safe he didn't care what it took. He trusted Andrew and felt confident that he was the man for the job. Jason left the house frustrated with her uncooperativeness. He would explain things to Sondra when she got home and hopefully she could talk some sense into her sister.

Sondra fretted anxiously when Jason told her about the incident. Her mood swings made it more difficult to reason with her lately. He had to calm her down and explain that Andrew would be there to protect her.

It was the first time that Sondra had learned about Andrew's background and she was furious that Jason didn't tell him sooner. She went on ranting and raving like a mad woman. Finally, Jason lost his temper and took her by the arm and ushered her up to their bedroom and slammed the door.

"Stop this ranting this instant! You have no idea what you are talking about. You will listen to me. Andrew will look after Jennifer whether you like it or not. In fact you do not even have a say in this. You are all my family and it is my job to protect all of you. She will be safe with Andrew around. She may not like it but I trust him to do this for me. Is that understood?" He angrily ran his hand though his hair.

"I'm sorry, Jason. I don't know what came over me. I guess I was just afraid. Of course, Andrew needs to protect Jennifer. I wish you had told me about him sooner. It would have been nice to know we had a Navy Seal on our team." She cracked a little smile hoping to catch him off guard.

That did the trick. He took her in his arms and held on to her tightly.

"I'm sorry I yelled too. I guess I too am afraid that something might happen to someone in my family. I take my job very seriously." He nuzzled her neck and started to kiss her. "Shall we kiss and make up?" he whispered into her ear.

She reached up and put her arms around his neck and gave him his answer with a long kiss.

~

Andrew rode into Parker Valley with a purpose. He took his horse to the barn and greeted Manuel with a nod. Cassie met him at the door and ushered him in tentatively.

She knew how Jennifer felt about having Andrew in the house and feared the conflict he would bring. He smiled at Cassie and took off his hat and put in on the coat rack at the door. He walked around the downstairs like he was casing the joint and Cassie felt trepidation. He sensed her fear and he gently offered to tell her of his background so that she could rest easy.

When she heard that he was a Navy Seal she smiled in relief. They would certainly be safe with him in the house. Andrew also told her that he would stay out of her way and just do his thing. The only request he had was that she tell him when and where she and Jennifer were going at all times. If she was to leave the premises he wanted to know about it, particularly Jennifer. If she failed to tell him he would hope that if Cassie noticed her leave that she would inform him immediately. Her protection was of the utmost. The first week would be the most critical.

She showed him where he would be sleeping and the bedrooms they were in, especially Jennifer's. They went downstairs and she got him a glass of lemonade.

When Jennifer came down the stairs, Andrew stood up and was introduced to her.

"We have met before, ma'am. It was at Mr. and Mrs. Nelson's wedding. I remember seeing you there." He looked at her without smiling.

He sized her up in a minute. She was hiding her anxiety and pretended to want to have nothing to do with him. That was just as well with him because he basically wanted nothing to do with her, except protect her life. It was better that they had a minimal relationship. She was spoiled and used to getting her way but he would not be thwarted in this.

"I was telling Miss Parker that the only thing I expect out of you is to listen to everything I tell you and do exactly what I say at the minute I tell you. I won't mince words. I want to know where and when you go out. If you go riding on the range expect that I will be there with you day or night. Please don't try to run from me, because you won't like the consequences. I will lock you in your bedroom if you try and escape from me. Is that understood?" He looked at her with narrowed steel gray eyes. "This is the only warning I will give you." He nodded to her and walked upstairs to his room.

"Well, wasn't that a fine introduction? I am calling Jason right now. I will not be spoken to in that manner especially from a hired hand. How dare he treat me that way?" She huffed off and went to use the phone. Cassie just shook her head and began to pray for peace to come upon their home.

She came back into the room with tears in her eyes.

"Jason told me that if I didn't do exactly what Andrew tells me to do that he will personally come and stand guard at my door when he locks me in it. I can't believe that this is happening to me. My freedom has been taken away from me. I might as well be in prison. Well, I won't stand for it." She ranted on and on. Cassie left the room because the tension was too great and she started to serve dinner.

They all sat down and had dinner together. Jennifer didn't speak at all and Andrew only complimented Cassie on the fine meal she put together. She sent up another prayer hoping that they all could get through this without a war.

Andrew was put to the test on the second day. Cassie came rushing to the front room when she heard screaming coming from Jennifer. Tommy ran from the office soon after her, expecting the worst, but only to find Andrew coming through the front door with Jennifer slung over his shoulder, her arms flailing and her feet kicking him. They watched as he brought his hand down and slapped her bottom when she kicked him too hard in the stomach. She cried out in protest of her handling. When he locked her in her room she screamed and cried even louder.

Cassie realized that Andrew must have put a lock on her door yesterday.

"I'm calling the police. How dare you manhandle me that way?" She screamed and kicked the door with her boots.

Andrew came down the stairs with a steely look in his eye.

"Two hours, next time it will be three. I told her I would only warn her once." He said to the two of them and left the house.

Cassie could only imagine what it was that she had done. Tommy smiled and shook his head in amazement. Someone was finally taking control of her.

She was still crying later when Cassie went upstairs. She was so upset that she hoped that the baby wouldn't be hurt. But she had had tantrums before and she seemed to be fine later.

After an hour of screaming, Cassie didn't know how much more she could take. She would call Sondra and perhaps Jennifer could stay with them. Her nerves were shot.

Tommy came out of the office and went into the kitchen just as she was about to make the call to Sondra.

"Sweetheart, why don't we just stay out of all this? This is probably the safest place for Jennifer to be. Her tantrums won't last long and I'm sure she has learned her lesson. Andrew seems to have a way with things. He will be the best protection she could possibly have. Let's just let him do his job. Why don't you give it a few more days and see what transpires?" He put his arm around her and hugged her. She cuddled into him and rested her head against his chest.

"What would I ever do without you?" She sighed as he held her.

The two hours were the longest in Cassie's life. The cries continued to come from upstairs and she could hear things thrown against the wall and broken. If she hadn't been locked in the room Cassie was angry enough to put her there herself. She hadn't realized what a brat she was. It must be the hormones.

When the two hours were up, Andrew went upstairs and unlocked the door. He stood in the doorway and looked at the mess that she had created. He looked at her with narrowed eyes and said evenly,

"Next time it will be three." And he walked away.

Jennifer just lay on the bed and cried into her pillow.

~

The next few days were quiet at the Parker Valley Ranch. Andrew had made his point and Jennifer wasn't speaking to anyone. She just walked around acting like the world was on her shoulders. She spoke to no one, especially Andrew. He started taking his meals in the bunk house with the boys and only came around the house to sleep.

Cassie's nerves were on edge. She was delighted that Jennifer and Sondra were going into the city for their ultra sounds. Peace and quiet and a tension free house would be well appreciated. For Jennifer, it was the first time that she had smiled in two days. When Jason came to pick her up, Andrew walked out of the bunk house and got in the back seat. Jennifer refused to sit in the back seat with him. She turned to go away when Jason looked surprised and got out of the car and signaled her to come over. She walked back to the car and told him that she wouldn't sit in the car if Andrew was going with them.

Jason closed his eyes and took a deep breath. He knew that a confrontation was coming.

"Jennifer, get in the car."

"No, I'm not going if he is going." She folded her arms across her chest stubbornly.

"Jennifer, get in the car." His voice grew louder and more forceful.

"No." She walked away. He went after her and pulled her aside and asked her what was going on.

"That man is a complete bully and I will not go anywhere with him."

"Sweetheart, Andrew is there only for your protection. I am assuming by your attitude that the two of you have had a clash of wills. I told you earlier that you were to listen to everything he had to say and do exactly what he tells you. If you disobeyed the rules and parameters he set up, the punishment is not anyone's fault but yours. Stop acting like a child and come to terms with the fact that these are dangerous times and call for extreme measures. I am taking all the precautions I can for your safety. Now, before I lose my temper, get in the car."

Jennifer sized him up and realized that his limit couldn't be pushed anymore so she obediently opened the front door and asked Sondra to sit in the back. She was about to get out of the car when Jason put his foot down.

"Sondra darling, stay where you are and, Jennifer, get in the back seat." He looked at her with eyes that would not be negated.

Angrily, she opened the back door and slid in and slammed it hard behind her. She folded her arms and sat looking straight ahead.

"Now put on your seatbelt, please." His face held a slight smile.

Andrew just sat there looking straight ahead; acting like he was not paying much attention, but one could detect a slight smile.

The afternoon went smoothly. They met at the clinic at three o'clock for their appointments. Sondra was particularly excited. To see her baby for the first time was the most thrilling event of her life. They said at twelve weeks they could possibly tell the sex of the baby. She was hoping for a boy but would be delighted with a girl. She was the first to go in. She and Jason waited for the technician to enter the room.

The woman smiled and asked if this was their first child. They both nodded in unison. She lifted Sondra's shirt and squirted a liquid gel on her abdomen. The machine had a nozzle that she put on her stomach and you could see inside. Both were mesmerized by what they saw. You had to look closely but when the attendant smiled Sondra could see her tiny baby. She pointed out where the head was and the tiny arms and legs. Three or four minutes went by and the woman laughed and pointed to a tiny area.

"It's definitely a boy," she said.

Jason looked closer with a proud look on his face. "That's my boy!" He proudly touched Sondra's hair affectionately. She laughed and cried when she saw her little child moving around in her womb.

"It's a miracle, Jason. We are going to have a baby. Until you see it, sometimes you can't believe it."

The two of them came out of the room with delight written across their faces. They told Jennifer and Andrew that they were having a boy. Jennifer couldn't help but get caught up in the excitement and wondered if she was having a boy too.

When they called her name, she went into the room and Sondra went with her. The technician was a man but looked very professional. He asked the same question, if it was her first child. She nodded and felt the cool liquid gel on her tummy. As he waved the wand across her abdomen, he didn't smile. He was serious until he finally found what he was looking for. He seemed to lighten up after that. Sondra had watched him carefully and was praying that nothing was wrong with the baby by the way he acted.

The technician said very little during the episode and Sondra silently wished that the other woman was doing the test. This guy didn't really seem to know what he was doing. Sondra asked if he could tell the sex of the baby. He said that the way the baby was positioned, he couldn't tell. Jennifer seemed a little disappointed.

After the test, the technician asked Jennifer to step into the back office for a minute. He said the doctor probably would like to speak to her. Sondra was a little worried and told Jennifer to go in and wait for her because she wanted Jason to be there with them if there was bad news.

She left the room and went outside to find Jason. When they saw her come in the waiting room, Andrew asked where Jennifer was.

"I left her in the office because the doctor wanted to talk to her. Jason, I'm a little worried. I think something might be wrong with the baby. The technician looked concerned when he did the test." She was looking for comfort from her husband.

"Jennifer is in the room alone?" Andrew asked. He spoke to Jason. "Let's get in there. Something isn't right." They both took off urgently to find Jennifer and left a confused Sondra standing there.

They searched every room and couldn't find her. Andrew charged out the back door and, just as he opened it, he saw a black sedan taking off down the alleyway. Andrew was ready. He took out his gun from his waist band and knelt down and fired two clean shots at the tires. He was a sharp shooter so his aim was accurate and the car skidded and came to a standstill. The tires had burst and were going nowhere. The man ran out of the car and took off down the street. Andrew ran up to the car, threw open the backdoor and pulled Jennifer out.

She was shaking and crying all at once. She grabbed hold of Andrew and put her arms around his neck. He held her close and tried to calm her fears.

"It's okay now. You're going to be just fine." He tried to quiet her down.

Jason came up to them, relieved to see the situation was under control. They went back inside and called the police. Apparently, the technician wasn't a technician at all. Jennifer and Sondra tried to remember what he looked like and between the two of them they came up with some details. The police asked them to come down to the station and look at some pictures and talk to an artist that might be able to draw a likeness of the perpetrator.

Jennifer was still shaking when Jason put his arm around her.

"I'm sorry you had to go through this but we can't take any more chances. Now you know why Andrew is there to protect you. I hope you'll give him some slack," he said.

"I'm so sorry, Jason. I have been a fool. Can you ever forgive me for my attitude? I didn't mean to cause so much trouble." Tears flooded her eyes.

"It's not me that you should apologize to," he spoke clearly and walked away.

She went up to Andrew and shyly apologized to him for her childish behavior. Instead of accepting her apology he seized her arm angrily and took her aside.

"I told you specifically not to go anywhere alone. That means not even to an office. You could have been killed." His voice took on a harshness that Jennifer wasn't used to. "It's my job to protect you and if you go against my wishes I can't be responsible for the outcome." He walked away from her and left her with Jason. Jennifer just looked at him shocked that he would treat her that way. Jason just sat there and allowed him to chastise her. Sondra went to get up and comfort her sister but Jason held her back.

"She needs to think about this one, Sondra. Let's let them work it out. Hopefully, she will remember this incident and not let it happen again."

"Oh Jason, it really is my fault. I'm the one that left her alone." He held her and said they all needed to be more careful. Jason knew that his buddy would chastise himself for letting this happen.

Andrew went outside to cool himself down. Fear ran through his veins when he realized that Jennifer could have been taken. He had been in dozens of situations where he could act on impulse and not feel anything. Protecting his fellow Seals became second nature. He had been on missions that would curl your hair. He tried not to remember the times he had to take a life to save the life of another. But this was different. This young woman had no clue as to the danger she could have been in. It made him angry that he had been duped by that young punk of a technician. He was slipping up and wondered if he had lost his touch. He prayed silently to God to take care of Jennifer since he was so inadequate.

Chapter Fifteen

James couldn't believe that he had been at the Teen Challenge center for over three months. He had grown to appreciate Mary and Bill for their commitment to the center and to the men that resided there. Three more men had arrived after him and three men who were ready to leave left the center. There was a constant group of twenty gentlemen.

James grew and flourished into the man that God had created him to be. He led different Bible Study groups and was doing some counseling with one of the younger men who just came to the center a few weeks ago. A young man named Michael was alcohol and drug dependent and was still trying to detox and dry out. He had been fatherless most of his life and his mother was beside herself at what to do. She had heard of the center through her church and sent him there to see what they could do with him. She was at her wits' end.

James had taken a liking to him. He reminded him of himself. James was not fatherless but they suffered from the same insecurities. He had an older brother who could do no wrong. Both of them loved their brothers but felt they could never live up to their standards. They had shared their life stories together and found friendship in their trust of one another.

Mary was delighted with James's progress. He still captivated the group of men with his preaching and sense of humor. They asked him every night to do the devotions and practice his sermons. It came naturally to him. It was in his soul to tell others about the love of Jesus. She couldn't have been happier. She was arranging for him to talk at one of the local churches. They were a little hesitant at first because of the Teen Challenge background and who they ministered to but, when they heard him preach, they were astounded. He was to go this Sunday evening. They were planning an outing for all of them.

Secretly, Mary and Bill were planning a surprise for James. They had spoken to his brother, Jason, and invited them to the church that Sunday, but she didn't tell them that James would be the guest speaker.

James and Jonathan were still inseparable. The night they prayed together bonded them together forever. He was the one who encouraged him to preach the Word of God. When his spirit touched the heavens, it was easy for him to tell others of the love of Jesus. It just came naturally. He studied and prayed for hours on end each day. God had given him so much that he wanted to give back.

James thought of Jennifer constantly. He wondered if she had forgiven him for what he did to her. The last time he saw her, she looked better than he expected.

How could he have not seen how special she was? Jennifer was the type of girl that you brought home to meet mom and dad. She was a perfect candidate for a wife. She would be faithful and loving 'till death do us part.' She was innocent and full of life. James wished he could turn back the clock and change what had happened. She was the one person he had trouble forgiving himself for hurting. He prayed that God would take care of her and perhaps let him see her in the future.

The real reason he wanted so much to change was for her. She deserved better. Sometimes, at night, he could feel her in his arms. He had to pray that God would take the feeling of lust away and pour the truth into his spirit. He wanted to start over with her if that was even possible. But for now he would focus on getting healing for himself. There was so much he had to be thankful for.

This weekend was the week that family members could come and listen to some of their talks. He was praying that Sondra and Jason would come and see how far he had come. He was a little fearful of their reaction to them. He had done very little in the past to make his brother proud of him and he wanted to make an impression. As he sat in prayer one day, the Lord asked him if he wanted to please man or please God. That took him by surprise because it was his brother he was trying to please.

When he brought this up to Bill during his counseling session, he smiled and congratulated him on a milestone in his recovery.

"James, one of the problems of the past was that you wanted to please your brother. You looked up to him as you were growing up and saw the attention he was getting from your father and you thought that, if you emulated him, your father would be proud of you too. The only difference was that you were trying to please the wrong person. You grew up with some 'stinking thinking' and God wants to erase that from your thought process. So, many times we replace that 'stinking thinking' with 'stinking doing.' That is why people resort to drugs, alcohol and sex. It makes them feel good for a short time but it doesn't erase the disappointment and confusion. It will always be there until you come to terms with it. You were correct when you consulted God on the issue. Our only job is to please God. If we do not please man in the process, then that is too bad. We move on and continue to please the Father. When we finally reach our resting place in the hands of the Lord, it is only Him we have to answer to. Does that make any sense to you, James?" He had gentle smile that reached his eyes.

"Yes. I think that growing up I felt like I couldn't compete with Jason but now I understand that we had different gifting's. He was using his gifts and I was trying to cash in on them and failed, whereas I have a different gift that I am just becoming aware of. I think I under-stand perfectly. We are two different people and I was trying to be him. Now, if only I could concentrate on my gifting's, my life will become more secure and I will be happier." He thoughtfully tried to process the revelation.

"That's excellent, James! You have now passed round three of the course. Son, I am very proud of you!" He stood up and gave him a big bear hug. They both laughed together. "I believe you are ready to face your biggest challenge — your family."

James sat in the back of the room when the guests arrived that evening. He saw Sondra first and stood up to embrace her. That was when he noticed that she was pregnant. A huge smile lit up his face. He hugged her and congratulated her all at once. This was turning out to be one of the best days of his life. He was going to be an uncle for the second time. His sister Nicole just had a baby girl but he had not yet seen his niece. This was special. He felt close and bonded to Sondra and Jason. He shook Jason's hand and congratulated him also. It was a happy greeting. They sat down and talked about how things were going for James. He did not know that Jason and Sondra had been getting progress reports from Bill and Mary so he went on and on telling them in his own words the headway he was making. He spent a long time telling them how grateful he was that he had been encouraged to enter the program. God was beginning to change his life.

James handed an envelope to Sondra and asked her to give it to Jennifer. He had wanted to communicate with her but he was not permitted to make outside calls. He thought he could send his message of apology by letter.

Sondra was amazed at the change in her brother-in-law. She thanked God for this new man that was entering James. In a strange way, he was beginning to sound a bit like her husband. She listened intently to him when he talked about his life-changing spiritual journey. 'Perhaps he has become that man that God created him to be after all?' she thought to herself. She took a deep breath and shook her head and was amazed at the transformation He had made. 'God, you are wonderful'

Jason was a little more skeptical. He had heard similar words from his brother before. He needed to see some action behind the words before he could be convinced of his inner change. He would watch and wait.

The wait didn't last long. That night, they had the surprise of their lives. When Jason and Sondra went to church that evening, they listened to a man they hardly recognized as their brother. James captivated the congregation with his excitement and commitment to the Lord. By the end of his talk, practically everyone in the church felt convicted to go up to the front for prayer. It completely took Jason by surprise.

When Jason went up to the front, he took his brother in a big bear hug and told him how proud he was of him and what a gift the Lord had bestowed on him. Tears filled James's eyes and, for the first time, he felt a bond between himself and his brother. What a joy it was! He had waited his whole life to hear his brother say those words to him.

Sondra cried when she hugged him too. She could hardly speak as she was so taken by the Holy Spirit. James spent the rest of the night praying for the people of that church. They asked him to come back again sometime. This was the beginning of the transformation of James Allison Nelson into the world of evangelism.

After that night, he was asked by dozens of churches in the area to fill their pulpits. Word broke out that this young man had a gift to bring people back from their brokenness and turn them to the Father's love. His time alone with God was the pivot point to his success with His people. James began to understand that each of us had a key to unlock the chains that bound us from receiving the Father's love. He gave them the key that was purchased by the blood of the Lamb and helped them unlock the manacles that held them back from reaching their full potential. Lives began to change and voices began to sing the praises of Jesus through James's ministry.

Mary and Bill were pleased with his success but worried that it would hinder his total healing. He still had a long way to go with the program. There were 'sin areas' and ideals that hadn't been touched upon yet. Both of them felt that it was good for him to feel God's purpose in this life so they took special time to advance his training.

~

A transformation was beginning to form in Jennifer also. After her experience at the clinic, she went from a rebellious child to a woman who was about to become a mother. She too went back to reading the scriptures and tried to understand God's purpose for her life. She had great respect for Andrew because of the recent altercation they had. She did exactly as he instructed, and never went beyond the boundaries he had set up. She was not sent to her room again.

Andrew too noticed the change in Jennifer and was beginning to appreciate his young charge. She was kind, gentle and fun to be around. He started to worry that she was becoming too fond of him. He had seen it before. When there are life and death situations, sometimes the bond between the client and the guardian becomes too close. When you save someone's life, the person becomes over obligated to the protector and confuses gratitude for love. He kept her at arm's length and took his concerns to Jason. He wanted to be totally upfront with his boss.

Since the Johnson Project had gone through without a hitch after three weeks, Jason agreed with Andrew and felt it was safe for them all to go back to normal again. Because the one attempt at Jennifer's life was foiled, Jason felt the perpetrator had given up. He told everyone to be cautious and look for any signs that seemed abnormal. But he released Andrew from being Jennifer's protector to becoming a lead ranch hand again. Life seemed to slip back to normalcy.

Chapter Sixteen

Everyone at Willow Oaks and Parker Valley and the surrounding ranches were getting excited about 'family day.' Jason and his crew planned a special day for all the ranches in the area to come and celebrate. He believed that honoring his staff was important for morale purposes. They deserved a day off to come together and play. All the other ranches wanted to get in on the action so Jason went beyond his boundaries to the surrounding towns. He was surprised at the enthusiasm from his neighbors. After speaking with Pastor Jose, they thought it was a perfect time to do a fundraising for the orphanage. That was exactly what they would do. He hired a multitude of construction workers and caterers to build a Rodeo area that could hold hundreds of people.

They would have bull riding, barrel races, and bronco busting events just to name a few. Each contestant would pay a fee of fifty dollars to enter the contest, with all the proceeds going Pastor Jose's orphanage. Some scholarships would be issued to those who couldn't afford the cost. All the children in the orphanage were to be the guests of honor.

The excitement was building in the community and side bets were set up as to who would win what.

The last few weeks were a bustle of activity at Willow Oaks. Jason had put Sondra in charge of the design and construction of the site. She was thrilled. She organized what animals should be brought in for the event and where they would be kept. They built a huge arena on the back side of the barn far enough away so as not to disturb the running of the ranch. Her expertise in organization and her respect from the workers boded well for the project. Jason was proud of her as he watched her blossom, in more ways than one. She held a special glow as she went from site to site instructing and delegating.

They had two hundred contenders for the competitions. Some were enrolled in several events. Jennifer was in charge of putting together the events and posting them on the internet and billboards all over the town. She was a little worried that people would shun her because of her condition but she was so happy to be doing something that she blocked it from her mind. She decided if they had a problem with her it would be their problem, not hers. She was confident in who she was. After her incident at the clinic, she was just happy to be alive.

Everyone worked hard and tempers were flaring three days before the event. Sondra had to cool her irritation when she was told that some of the stands had to be eliminated because of time. She spoke directly to the contractor and urged him to consider working day and night on the project. He explained that his men were tired and there just wasn't enough time to complete it. She went to task and had Jason bring in special workers from Dallas. The cost would go way over budget but she thought it would be worth it and Jason agreed.

Cassie was working on the concession stands to sell hot dogs and hamburgers for the kids and arranging the barbecue for the ribs and the big old T-bone steaks and Texas fries for the rest. There would be a dance and a buffet dinner later that night. Roberta was in charge of the caterers for that evening. Everything was under control and the excitement was building. It would be a day filled with fun and everyone was full of anticipation.

Jennifer woke the next morning with a splitting headache. She blamed the tension in her neck and lower back on her lack of sleep and lifting too much. When she started to get out of bed she looked down and the sheets were covered with blood.

"Oh, my God! Help me Lord!" She screamed for Cassie with a blood curdling yell. Cassie flew from her bed into her room to see what could be wrong. When she saw the blood, she tried to calm herself and Jennifer at the same time.

"It's okay, sweetheart. Sometimes this occurs. You are almost four months pregnant and this sometimes happens. Let's just calm ourselves down and I'll call an ambulance."

Jennifer started shaking and crying all at once. Cassie flew downstairs and called an ambulance and called Doctor Martin. He answered the phone when he found out from the caller ID that it was Cassie.

He told her not to panic and said he would meet them at the hospital. It was probably something minor. He told her that it sometimes occurs.

Cassie immediately called Sondra. She said she would be there in fifteen minutes. The ambulance arrived before Sondra and Jason, and when they drove up in the driveway, the seriousness of the situation settled in. Jason ran into the house before Sondra and got there as they were bringing Jennifer out the door.

"Hi, sweetheart, everything is going to be okay. We are here with you. We will meet you at the hospital. We will be right behind you." He held her hand as they carried her out.

Sondra was there to see her sister being put in the ambulance. Cassie stepped in behind her. She smiled at Sondra and said she talked to Dr. Martin and he would meet them at the hospital.

"He said not to worry, that it sometimes happens. Keep praying." She started getting teary eyed.

"We will, Cassie. Give Jennifer a kiss for me," she added in a panic, afraid that she too might break out in tears. Jason held her tightly as they watched the ambulance leave with Jennifer tucked inside.

As Sondra got in the car, Jason held her hand and asked if they could pray for Jennifer. Sondra held on to him and he prayed gently.

"Father we don't know what is wrong with Jennifer's baby but we know that you know all things. We have faith Lord that you are in control of what is going on here. Take care of our Jennifer. She is in your hands Father. Give us the strength to walk through this door and keep us focused on you. You are the King of Kings and Lord of Lords. We love you, Jesus. Amen." Sondra continued to hang on to him for strength and they took off towards the hospital.

As Jason and Sondra entered the emergency room, they were confronted by a bustle of activity. Soon after they arrived, Claira came rushing through the door. She had left for the shop earlier that morning to do some catch up work and came as quickly as she could.

"Has anyone heard anything yet?" she asked, her voice sounding strained.

Cassie came up to the three of them and smiled weakly.

"I haven't heard from Doctor Martin yet but I saw him briefly when he came in. He said not to worry. They have everything under control. They put an obstetrician in charge of her care as soon as we arrived. Let's go and sit down."

They all sat down to wait for any word from the doctors. It wasn't until at least an hour later that Doctor Martin came in the waiting room. He had a big smile on his face that eased the tension on all of them.

"She is doing just fine. She is resting now. We gave her a slight sedative. She has lost a lot of blood so we had to give her a transfusion. The baby is fine. There was a slight rupture of the uterus but miraculously after an ultra sound it seemed to have mended itself. I'm sure you were all praying. This kind of thing happens rarely but it was caught in time. You can take her home as soon as we finish the paper work." He smiled happily and left them.

They all breathed a sigh of relief. No one spoke for a few minutes. All of a sudden, Sondra broke into tears. Jason took her aside and held her close, trying to be as comforting as possible. He knew that she was exhausted mentally, worrying about Jennifer. He hoped she wasn't stressing out baby Jacob too much. He tried to calm her down as much as possible.

Claira smiled happily at Cassie and decided to go back to work. "Give Jennifer a kiss for me and tell her I will see her tonight with a new nightgown and house-coat. She deserves a little something special for all she's been through." She hugged Cassie and Sondra and Jason and left feeling much better.

When she got home, Jennifer rested that day and was feeling much better the next. Jason wondered whether she should attend the 'family day' or not. He was worried about overexertion on her part. Sondra told him that she would take care of her. They would spend most of the day sitting and watching the festivities. Everything was being taken care of and they were not needed. That helped put Jason's mind at rest.

"I hope you both will do just that, sweetheart. I don't want either of my girls stressing out over anything tomorrow. Do you promise?" he asked.

"Yes, Jason. I will take care of Jennifer. She scared me half to death. I don't want anything to happen to her or the baby. I'm just so thankful that everything is alright." She breathed a sigh of relief.

Chapter Seventeen

The day started with breakfast in bed. Roberta surprised them by bringing a tray to their bedroom. It was full of toast, bacon and eggs and Sondra's special drink.

The two of them ate happily and discussed the start of the day's festivities. Soon, Willow Oaks would be full of excited and cheerful contestants. Sondra could hardly wait for the activities to begin. She especially was looking forward to the Bronco Riding competition. Jason was enrolled in this contest. She wanted to see her man take home the prize. Besides, she loved to see him ride a horse and compete.

Jennifer came later that morning excited about the upcoming day. She looked wonderful. Her complexion was beautiful and silky smooth. Her blonde hair was thick and rich looking. She wore it shoulder length but today she had it tied up in an attractive ponytail. Being pregnant gave her a certain glow that only comes from motherhood. She was not showing very much so her clothes still fit perfectly. The only thing was that she wore them a little looser in the abdomen.

Sondra was showing much more and was mortified when she couldn't get into her riding clothes. She was able to get Claira, her gifted seamstress sister, to alter her favorite outfits. All she showed was a little pooch in her stomach. She was determined to stay out of maternity clothes for as long as possible. But secretly, she was anxious for her little Jacob to grow big and strong, no matter how large she got.

Jason held her stomach every evening and prayed over their unborn child. Jason took his fatherhood very seriously. He cared for his precious wife and child like crystal glass.

They all headed out to the arena that Sondra had masterminded over the last three weeks. It had come together with skill and perseverance. There were ten rows of portable stands surrounding the area that was a little less than half the size of a football field. There were chutes with swinging doors built into the side where they could let the bulls into the dirt field. Large barrels sat strategically throughout the field for the barrel races. It appeared to be the most popular event. There was a tower built into the structure where the announcer of the races could oversee the ring and broadcast the winners. Sondra was proud of the job she had done of overseeing the construction.

They met Andrew as they entered the arena. He was head of the security department for the event. Jason had hired a security firm out of Dallas to help Andrew secure the area. Andrew would not allow any weapons, which included guns or ammo, on the premises. He monitored and watched everyone who came through the entrance.

Anyone looking suspicious would be confronted. So far, all was well. He gave Jason and Sondra a nod and a half smile to Jennifer as they walked into the arena.

The crowds started coming one at a time in their trucks, usually hauling a horse trailer. The stable hands were ready to greet their guests and show them where to put their mounts. There was a bustle of activity as the spectators appeared from all over.

Roberta had coffee stands and donuts ready for the contestants and spectators. Jennifer and Sondra stayed to help her distribute food and drink to the early birds. They laughed and enjoyed greeting people from all over the countryside. They were excited about meeting the new Mrs. Nelson, and when they found out she was expecting they were equally happy. Some raised their eyebrows but those who knew Sondra were ecstatic.

The mood was festive and exciting as the first contestants for the barrel races got ready. Jennifer and Sondra settled into their seats as they watched the competition. She got up and waved as Pastor Jose and some of the orphan children came to watch the barrel races. They started to come their way when they saw her. Little Maria saw Sondra and ran ahead to join her. Sondra hugged her and swung her around when she reached her.

"Hello, sweetheart. You look especially pretty today. I love your hair in braids. You look like a ballerina." She hugged her again and they all sat down together to watch the contest.

The morning went by quickly and Jennifer was starting to get hungry. She was craving pickles.

"Why don't we go and get a hot dog or a hamburger and you can have all the pickles you want." Sondra laughed at her sister as they stood up to leave. She took Maria's hand and Jennifer walked with the other children to the food stands.

"Sondra, I have to run to the bathroom. Will you watch the children for a minute and I will be right back?" She left her and headed for the portable washrooms.

Sondra took all the children to see Roberta at the food stand. She happily fed them barbecued hot dogs and some of the children wanted chicken burgers. They ate happily. Sondra watched the children with their polite manners sit quietly at one of the picnic tables.

She hadn't realized that half an hour had gone by and Jennifer hadn't returned from going to the bathroom. She looked around hesitantly wondering where her sister had gone to. She thought she probably stopped to talk to someone on the way.

Out of the corner of her eye she thought she had seen a familiar face. When she looked closer, that face took on shape. It looked like the technician at the clinic where Jennifer was almost abducted. He disappeared into the crowd and Sondra lost sight of him. She jumped up quickly and asked the lady sitting next to her to watch the children. She ran to try and find Jason.

"Dear God, help me!" she prayed as she looked for her husband. She ran up and down the aisle of people shouting for Jason. People looked at her as if she had lost her mind. Someone pointed in a direction and she caught sight of her husband.

"Jason!" she shouted above the noise of the crowd. He stopped what he was doing and quickly ran to her side.

"Sondra, what's wrong?" He looked into her frightened face. She could hardly catch her breath.

"Jennifer is missing. I think I saw that technician that tried to take Jennifer from the clinic." She spoke between panicky gulps.

"Calm down, sweetheart. Tell me from the beginning what happened." He tried to calm his wife so he could get the facts.

"Jennifer went to go to the bathroom about half an hour ago and hasn't returned. When I looked through the crowds, I think I saw that man. Oh Jason, what if he has taken Jennifer?" She started to cry.

Jason immediately took her hand and quickly went through the crowds to find Andrew. He was still at the entrance to the arena checking to make sure things were secure. Jason whispered to him about Jennifer's disappearance. He immediately went into action. All the security guards were sent to all parts of the area to look for her. He specifically went to where all the cars and trucks were parked to see if any had recently left the ranch. He was told by the attendant that only a few people had left but he didn't recognize any of them. He would have seen Jennifer if she was among them.

The next hour or two was spent looking for her. The crowd helped when they were alerted that she had disappeared. All the competitions stopped while everyone searched the area.

Sondra's fear grew into a nightmare as each minute ticked by. No one had seen Jennifer, or the man who was described by Sondra. They could only suspect the worst.

Jason went into the house to call the police after the initial search. He thought the sooner they could find clues to her disappearance the faster she would be found. They arrived soon after his call.

The police detective questioned everyone at the 'family day' outing. They found nothing suspicious with the guests on the premises. They spoke to the ranch hands who looked after the horses and the coming and going of vehicles. Nothing out of the ordinary was discovered there. It was if she had disappeared into thin air.

The competitions continued but there was lacking an enthusiasm as everyone was concerned for the whereabouts of Jennifer. Andrew kept a straight face but Sondra could see the worry behind his eyes. She knew that look as she had seen it before. Sondra wondered secretly if there wasn't a slight attraction for her younger sister. He was a professional and it was hard for him to show emotion but, in a split second, Sondra could see the apprehension building. He was really concerned for her safely. That alone gave Sondra chills.

"I'm going to make a few calls." Andrew walked towards the house.

It was quiet as he stepped into the foyer. The coolness of the air-conditioning was refreshing as he walked further into the beautifully decorated front room. Its elegance stood out beside this young man dressed in dusty jeans and cowboy boots. He had taken his Stetson Hat off as a habit when he entered the house. He brushed back his dark hair to keep it out of his tanned face. The telephone was in the hallway beside the stairway. Just as he reached it he heard a creak in the floor boards of the stairs. He looked up only to find Jennifer sleepily descending the staircase. Relief spread across his face and he grinned briefly before it turned into dark fury as she reached the bottom step.

She looked at him and rubbed the sleep out of her eyes. That was when she noticed the furious look on his face. He swung her around to face him with both hands grabbing her arms. He gave her a rough shake.

"Where the heck have you been, young lady? Do you have any idea the commotion you have caused us? You are the most inconsiderate child I have ever met in my whole life. We have been worried sick about you." He spoke through clenched teeth.

"Excuse me? I don't know what you are talking about. And get your hands off me!" she cried, trying to remove herself from his grasp. He only gripped her firmer.

"The whole town is out looking for you at this moment. The police have been here and there is an Amber Alert out for you and you dare to give me that high handed attitude?" He gave her a light shake again.

He let her go right after that, afraid of what he might do to her. He then walked abruptly out the front door, leaving a stunned Jennifer to comprehend what he told her.

Horrified, she stood there afraid of what to do next. She was still standing there when Sondra ran into the house and gave her a huge hug.

"Thank God you are safe, Jennifer. We thought you had been abducted. Where have you been?"

"I came in to go to the bathroom, because all the stalls outside were busy, and I was tired and decided to lie down in your spare bedroom." She started to cry realizing how foolish she had been. "I had no idea that it would cause such an uproar. I'm so sorry, Sondra. I should have told you. Everyone must hate me. I have never seen Andrew so angry. He must hate me too." She had a frightened look on her face.

"I think that Andrew was so frightened that you had been kidnapped again that he reacted just like men react. They don't know how to handle their own emotion, so they take it out on the ones they care about. He wouldn't have been upset with you, Jennifer, if he didn't like you."

Just at that moment, Jason came in with Cassie, Claira and Roberta on his heels. The girls shouted for joy when they saw her. They led her outside where everyone was waiting. They cheered when they saw her. Everyone was hugging everyone. They were all so glad that she was okay.

Jason made the call to the police station to tell them she was alive and well. After that, he went to find Andrew, after Sondra had filled him in on his handling of Jennifer. He had cooled off a little when Jason confronted him.

He smiled as he sat down on the bench beside him. "I can get pretty angry and it's hard to control sometimes but, with God's help, we men can accomplish anything." He waited for the words to settle in. Andrew just sat there chewing on a piece of hay, not willing to admit to anything. He had calmed himself down. "You must really care for her." He looked Andrew in the eyes as he got up to leave. "Thanks for caring, buddy." He patted him on the back.

Andrew just sat there digesting his feelings and emotions for the young girl who was driving him crazy.

The competitions started back up, soon after that, and winners were called and trophies were handed out. Before the end of the afternoon, everyone had forgotten about Jennifer's disappearance and people were ready for the barbecue and dance.

The orphan children could hardly wait for the festivities to begin. Little Maria had not left Sondra's side as they walked and talked together all afternoon. Sondra was becoming attached to this little darling. She was only three years old but could talk a blue streak. Only Sondra could understand everything she was saying. They chatted on and on about nothing in particular.

Jason stood back and watched his wife as she bent down to kiss Maria's knee when she fell and got a cut.

The joy on the little one's face melted Jason's heart. They were like two peas in a pod. He wondered the fate of their little charge. He was praying that Sondra would become so attached to her that they would finally be able to adopt her. He would be patient and wait for Sondra to make that decision. He was already on board.

They had erected a huge tent on the property that would house all their guests. Tables with red checkered tablecloths made it look festive.

Pastor Jose thanked everyone for their contribution to this successful fundraising day and he blessed the food before the first bite of roast beef was taken. Everyone devoured the delicious food like it would be their last meal. Roberta had outdone herself. After every last person was fed, the dancing would begin.

The dance floor was set up in the middle and, when they were given the okay, the fiddlers began to play. After an old fashioned hoe-down, the country band came in to play for the younger folks. There was line dancing and traditional waltzes. There was a mix for everyone.

Jennifer was exhausted by the end of the day. She was tapped on the shoulder and when she looked up Andrew was there.

"May I have this dance?" His voice was without expression.

Jennifer hesitated but decided to accept his offer. He guided her along the dance floor with expert moves. She glided along with him. He spoke in her ear halfway through the dance.

"I'm sorry that you felt I threatened you, Jennifer. Please forgive me. I was relieved and upset at the same time," he said, without apology, as he swung her around the dance floor.

Jennifer said nothing for she was startled by his admission and surprised at his skill on the dance floor. 'There was more to this cowboy than meets the eye,' she thought to herself. In his arms, she felt secure and protected. It was a new feeling for her and she wondered where it came from. She closed her eyes and flowed with the music as he expertly guided her. She didn't realize that the dance had ended until he came to an abrupt halt and she ran into him.

"I'm sorry," she confessed with a red face as she opened her eyes. She was wearing her emotions on her face. He smiled down at her and gently ushered her off the floor before they became a spectacle. He took her outside the tent for a breath of fresh air and before she could utter a word, he pulled her towards him and bent down and kissed her lips firmly and with purpose. She melted against him as her stomach did a flip flop.

'Oh God, he tastes so good,' she thought.

He then abruptly turned and went to the bunk house. 'What a strange thing to do,' she surmised as she watched him saunter away. She gulped and wondered what had just happened.

The 'family day' was a huge success. All the ranchers and neighbors raved about the wonderful time they had. They hoped that it would be a yearly event. Jason promised that as long as he was there it would be.

Chapter Eighteen

Their first holiday together came and went that year with much celebration. Sondra enjoyed decorating the ranch and holding the most lavish but down home Christmas parties. New Year's Eve was a quiet affair as they brought in the New Year in front of the fire place, drinking hot chocolate. Roberta was off visiting her sister for the holidays so Sondra was in charge of the kitchen. Jason was actually surprised by her skill. That night, they were happy just being together.

Cassie and Tommy went to the local parties and dragged Jennifer along with them. Claira was always too busy working in her shop to go to any of the functions. Sondra worried that she was working too hard. Her customers were demanding and long hours were spent designing outfits for the holidays. She told them that the first year in business was always the hardest. She had to establish her customers and make them long term. Sondra missed her sister Claira but she understood her passion for her work.

The winter days passed quickly and Sondra and Jennifer grew in girth with their respective pregnancies.

Sondra woke up cranky and unreasonable. Being six months pregnant was not easy for her. She was blossoming in the abdomen too much for her liking. Jason learned to ignore her in the mornings, until she had her breakfast. She had given up coffee as soon as she found out she was pregnant and replaced it with an energy drink of fruits and vegetables mixed in a blender. Roberta fixed her drink first thing in the morning and would bring it to her by seven thirty.

Just as she was about to enter the bedroom with a gentle knock, Roberta hesitated when she heard Sondra and Jason arguing.

"Don't argue with me, Sondra! Just do as I ask," he ordered.

"But it's not a reasonable request. I feel just fine and the doctor told me I could do the things I always do. You have no right to forbid me to ride today. In fact you have no right to forbid me to do anything. Do you think I am a child? That I can't make proper decisions for myself? How dare you treat me this way?" She stomped her foot in frustration.

"Sondra, I told you I spoke to Doctor Martin and he agreed with me that you should use discretion when it comes to doing strenuous activity. I'm only thinking of you and Jacob."

"Don't use our baby as an excuse to boss me around," she snapped back when he turned away from her.

Jason was about to lose his temper when Roberta decided to knock on the door. He took a deep breath and walked out of the door that she just opened. He looked at Roberta and shrugged his shoulders.

"You heard me, Sondra." He spoke firmly as he left the room.

"Oh, that man! Roberta, is he always this obstinate? I am about ready to scream."

Roberta walked into the room and handed Sondra her drink. "You have to learn how to handle him, my dear. I found that, if you pick your battles, you have fewer arguments. If it is something you really want to win, go for it and stress your opinions until you win. If not, just let it go and let them think they win. It's usually a win, win situation." She started straightening up the room. "We women have to learn to be creative. But be sensible too, Sondra. Are you sure he is not right about you riding on the range today? It's rough out there."

"So, you did hear our disagreement?" She paused and thought carefully. "I have been riding since I was three years old. Being pregnant is not being handicapped. I think I will be fine, Roberta. It's not like I am nine months pregnant. I'm not about to pop." She looked down at her abdomen and laughed.

"You are probably right, dear. But it is getting very cold out there. After all, it is the beginning of February. My advice is not to go against Jason's wishes. I have a feeling you won't fare very well if you do, especially if he wants to win this one."

"I'm not afraid of Jason, Roberta. I am my own woman and he knows it. I would never do anything to harm little Jacob." She looked around the room for her socks. "Thank you for my drink. It is always appreciated, as well as your advice."

Sondra got dressed in warm riding clothes and went out to the barn to talk to Jason one more time. She wanted to win this battle because it was outside on the range where Sondra was able to relax and appreciate life. She couldn't imagine not being able to ride whenever she wanted to. It was unrealistic of Jason to tell her she couldn't. She would try to compromise.

Jason saw her coming and groaned. He knew she was on the warpath and he wanted desperately to get away. He didn't want her to make a scene.

"Hello, darling. What can I do for you?" He took her arm and started walking out of the earshot of his men.

"Are you handling me, Jason?" she whispered silkily.

"I don't know what you are talking about." He smiled as he continued to walk out of the barn getting more irritated with her banter.

He turned to face her and his face looked defeated. "Sondra, I don't want to argue with you today. I really worry about you and I don't want you to take any chances. Your blood pressure is higher than normal and Doctor Martin was worried that there might be some complications. I just want you to see reason. I don't want what happened to Jennifer to happen to you."

"Is that what is bothering you Jason? I agree with you. What if I rode slowly with one of the men? He could stay with me the whole time and see that nothing happens. And, if there is a problem, he will be there to help me. What do you say? I feel absolutely great and it would be good for me to get out in the fresh air. It is such a beautiful winter day, sweetheart." She looked at him convincingly, with clear blue eyes and a sassy smile.

He grimaced. How could he refuse her enchanting smile? "Okay. But it will be on my terms. I worry about you. I will send Andrew out with you. He has had some experience with the Parker girls and won't take any nonsense. Agreed?"

"I agree." She smiled happily. "Thank you, darling. I do love you."

She ran into the barn skipping and jumping for joy while Jason laughed.

When he found Andrew and asked him for the favor, he didn't look too excited about taking Sondra out for a ride but he was a disciplined man of few words. Sondra was just happy to be out in the fresh air on Sasha. The two rode out together with Jason watching them with his hands on his hips.

"Take care of my girl, Andrew," he called after them. Andrew just waved his hand. As soon as they left the ranch, Sondra galloped out onto the grassy fields as soon as she could. It took Andrew by surprise and he galloped after her, shaking his head. Another independent woman was in his care. He sighed and prayed briefly for their safely.

Sondra hadn't been on her horse for a few days and was oblivious to what was going on around her. She even forgot that Andrew was behind her. She didn't care. She was free from all the cares of the world. She galloped faster and faster feeling the wind blow through her hair.

Andrew watched her take off at a fast pace and admired her horsemanship. She was probably the most accomplished horsewoman he had ever met. She looked like a vision with her long blond hair flowing with the wind as she rode one with her horse. He rode faster to keep up with her. He pursed his lips together, not exactly happy about her riding as fast as she was but he didn't argue. She slowed down as soon as she reached a wooded area. Andrew rode with her side by side.

"Thank you, Andrew, for agreeing to babysit me. You really don't need to but thank you anyway."

He just tipped his hat to her, in acknowledgement. They rode in silence for about another half an hour. She was the happiest she had been in a long time.

Andrew started to relax as soon as they came to the little lake. It was his favorite place to come, to unwind from the day's troubles.

Sondra got off her horse and sat down beside the water's edge. Andrew stayed on his mount and waited for her.

"Why don't you come and sit down here with me, Andrew?"

He got off his horse, and stood beside her, watching the ripples on the lake.

"Did you know that this is where Jason proposed to me?" Her voice was getting whimsical.

He just looked at her thoughtfully.

"Don't you ever speak? I don't bite."

"Yes ma'am," he answered.

"Jason was very romantic when he asked me to marry him. He set up a beautiful table, with crystal glasses, silver, and candles. It was the most romantic time of my life." She stared at the water remembering that wonderful day. "Did you know that Jason was that romantic, Andrew?"

"No ma'am," he answered.

Sondra laughed. "You are a man of few words, Andrew Walker."

He just grunted. They watched the water ripple as the cool wind whistled across the lake. The sun settled gently upon its surface looking like diamonds sparkling throughout its wake. Sondra gazed upon its serene beauty.

"Did I ever thank you for saving my baby sister? You really impressed me. I like having you around, Andrew." They sat in silence for a little awhile.

"Do you care about my sister, Andrew?" she asked right out of the blue. She turned and looked him straight in the eye.

He looked away awkwardly and gulped before he answered. She had always made him feel comfortable in her presence but her straight forward question was one he wrestled with.

"I don't know, Mrs. Nelson. All I know is that, at that moment, I was worried sick about her and I felt so helpless and I don't like feeling helpless. At times, she drives me crazy with her lackadaisical attitude. And then I realize that she is really only a child."

Sondra absorbed what he had said and smiled to herself. 'He has caught the love bug.'

They left that area soon after and Sondra spent time checking up on her cattle. It was a joyous time for her. She loved to be free to roam the wide open range. It was the land that belonged to Jason and her. She could hardly believe that she was married to this land baron who adored her. When it was time for them to leave, she let out a yelp of joy and took off through the open pastures homeward. Andrew followed her and shook his head at her impulsiveness. He admired her for her candor and her zest for life.

Chapter Nineteen

Winter was mild that year at Willow Oaks and Parker Valley. Jennifer was blossoming with the new life that was inside her. She was beginning to feel alive with the hope of a new baby that tests revealed would be a girl who was soon to be born. Doctor Martin advised her to go slowly up and down the stairs and not to do anything strenuous like lifting or riding.

She put up an argument with Jason about riding her gentle horse, Candy, but he won that battle. She realized that it was a small price to pay for a healthy child. Her horse was ridden from time to time by the ranch hands. She spent many hours talking and walking Candy around the bull pit. She loved her horse. She had been given Candy by her father when she turned sixteen. It was a joyous day in her life.

Jennifer and her father had been very close. When he and her mother died in the plane crash, she took it extremely hard. Being the youngest daughter of four girls, she was the one who stole her daddy's heart. The other girls were independent and were self-sufficient by their mother's hand. She was more lenient on her youngest daughter as it was just easier not to argue.

Jennifer didn't have to spend hours at the piano or learning how to sew. She was more interested in getting her degree at the university in counseling so that she could help others overcome their emotional obstacles. With her recent incident with James, she realized just how much other women would need her help. She planned to go back to college after the baby was born. She struggled with whether she should give her little girl up for adoption or raise her herself. She was, however, leaning towards keeping her and raising her on her own.

She, like Sondra, loved to ride and work on the ranch. She helped Sondra whenever she could. Her independent spirit showed when she rode with the cowboys on the range, branding and rounding up their cattle. They loved her as their little sister. They were careful how they treated her, now that she was carrying a baby. They were more vigilant and protective towards her than Jason was. Secretly, she loved all the attention. She was growing in more ways than one.

James too was growing. Mary and Bill were excited with the way he was taking responsibility for himself. He shared his testimony every Sunday at different churches that invited him to preach. They were astounded at the popularity of his charismatic charm. He was called the 'Handsome Preacher', due to his striking good looks and brilliant smile. He captivated the hearts of the young and old alike. Since he started preaching at the churches, literally thousands of people had given their lives to Christ. He struck a chord in the hearts of many.

James sincere outlook about his faith encouraged others to look at themselves and make a decision.

Mary was cultivating James to be the next young evangelist to hit the Christian world. He had invitations to go on TBN and the 700 Club to give his testimony. And he was becoming popular among the young Christian music world.

Mary was beginning to wonder if James was ready to leave their care and go out on his own. She had talked to his brother, Jason, many times during the last month and he agreed that perhaps they had done their job and he was ready to face the world and its temptations. Graduation would be set for the fifth and he would be home before Valentine's Day.

Sondra was concerned about how Jennifer would react to his homecoming and how James would react to her. They had not told him yet that Jennifer was having his baby. They didn't want anything to interfere with his healing and growth. They planned to tell him on his graduation day and they both wondered how he would handle the news that he was going to be a father.

Mary had called earlier that day and had thought it would be a very good idea for them to meet before graduation so that some closure could be made with regards to what James had done to Jennifer. Forgiveness was a tremendous part of his healing and for her also.

Sondra wondered how Jennifer would feel about meeting James this weekend. Jason thought it was an excellent idea for her to visually see the changes God had made in him. And, on the other hand, he had a right to know about his child, without it being sprung on him at his graduation. There was no doubt that Jennifer was pregnant. With less than two months to go, she looked like she was carrying a basketball. Her round stomach was very visible.

Jennifer came to the door and greeted her sister with open arms. The two of them looked like two peas in a pod. They laughed when their stomachs touched as they could barely get their arms around each other. Jason looked a little more serious when he entered and Jennifer wondered what was on their minds.

"Come and sit down. Cassie is making some cocoa for us." They sat in the living room.

"We won't stay long, Jennifer. We have a request for you. You don't have to answer right away but we would like you to think about it and pray about it."

"What is it?"

Jason leaned in a little closer to her before he explained the situation.

"James will be graduating next weekend. They feel that he has done a remarkable job in the Teen Challenge program. Mary and Bill feel that he is ready to face the world and be on his own again. They would like you to come to the center this weekend and meet with James." He waited to analyze her reception to the idea.

She just stared at them puzzled. "Does he know about the baby?" She protectively ran her hand around her stomach.

"No. We haven't told him because we didn't want anything to keep him from staying at the center. We felt you were safe in our care and he was safe in theirs."

"Okay. That makes sense to me. When do we go?"

Jason smiled at his sister-in-law. She had surprised both of them with her mature outlook.

"Are you sure you are okay with him knowing about the baby?" Sondra asked.

"I think so, Sondra. After all, he is the father. He has a right to know about her." She paused. "Do you think he will freak out when he finds out?"

"I don't know. He will probably feel remorse about you having to go through this because of his actions towards you. Other than that, I can't say how he will react."

Jennifer nodded quietly.

They all agreed that they would go in the morning. Jason would contact Mary that evening to set it up. They stayed and prayed together that all would go as God had planned.

~

Jennifer woke that morning with a headache. She had been up most of the night worrying about the meeting with James. How was he going to feel about being a father? She knew that he would be shocked and perhaps upset that he wasn't told earlier.

"Oh God," she prayed "give me the words and strength to face James. I felt so ashamed of the way I acted with him Lord. I forgive him Father for his actions. I don't want him to feel responsible for me Lord, or my baby. I just want what you want, Father. Please show me what to do."

She dressed warmly and waited for Jason and Sondra to pick her up. As she walked down the stairs, Cassie met her with a smile.

"Good morning, 'my love.'" She greeted her with a plate of pancakes and fruit. "I made your favorite this morning. You need to eat something to keep your strength up for the ride. I made you, Jason and Sondra some hot chocolate to take with you in the car."

Jennifer smiled for the first time that day thankful that her sister was so intuitive. That would keep her mind off their mission this morning. The drive only took an hour and a half. They arrived on time with Mary and Bill and James waiting for them in the living room. They were alone, with no distractions when Jason, Sondra and Jennifer entered. A fire was blazing in the fireplace which gave the atmosphere a cozy feeling. But Jennifer's eyes were only on James when she walked through the door. He stood up and greeted her with a big smile on his face but kept his distance next to the fire.

When she took off her coat, his eyes trailed down to her stomach. You could hardly mistake what he saw. He gulped and his smile turned to surprise when he comprehended what had happened. He put his hand on his mouth and groaned visibly. Tears came to his eyes when he looked at her.

"Oh my God, Jennifer, why didn't someone tell me?" He looked at his brother. "I am so sorry. Can you ever forgive me?" He choked the words out as he came forward to hold her. "Are you okay? Why didn't you tell me? I would have helped you some way, any way I could. Oh, I am so sorry," he repeated over and over as he held her.

She gently pushed him away. "It's okay, James. It was my decision to keep this from you. I was in good hands with my family. We wanted you to give everything you had to this ministry, James, without distractions."

"But I could have done something. You have had to go through this all by yourself. Please forgive me for what I did to you, Jennifer." He looked her in the eye. I have done some terrible things in my past and it's hard to believe we have a God who can forgive all those things. I hope you can too."

"Of course I forgive you, James. That was all in the past. There is a wonderful future we have to look forward to." She paused slightly, looked down and put her hand on her stomach. "God has forgiven me too, James. You were not the only guilty party in this. My rebellion has gotten me into a lot of trouble too. We both had a lot to learn. We must thank God that we learned it so quickly but, unfortunately, our lesson didn't come without consequences that not only we have to live with but our child will have to live with also."

When she turned around, she noticed that they were alone in the room. She was grateful to be able to talk to James by herself. Thankfully, her shame would not be shared with others looking on.

"I know this comes as a shock and a surprise to you, James, but I don't want you to think that you have to do anything about it. I have decided to raise her by myself. I don't want you to think you have to be a part in that. You have a future it seems in the ministry. You will be wonderful, James. I always knew you had a special gift. God will really use you to do marvelous things. We will be just fine so I don't want you to worry about us. My family has been a wonderful support," she rambled on.

He stopped her with a finger on her lips. He sat her down on the sofa and turned to face her.

"It's a girl? A girl...I can't believe I'm going to be a father. However, it does come as a surprise and a shock to me that you would be okay raising her by yourself." He looked her in the eye and said sadly, "I wish I could have shared this with you Jennifer. It wasn't fair that you had to do this alone. I'm so sorry." He choked up again. "But I want to make this right with you. Tell me how I can help. I will do anything. Do you think that we should get married? I don't know if you will even have me for the scum bag that I've been?"

She stopped him with a finger on his lips and laughed.

"Let's just give this some time to settle in, okay? Then we can decide what God wants us to do about it. Does that make sense?"

James hugged her after that and agreed that they would pray and ask God for His perfect plan for them and the new life that was soon to come into this world.

"I just can't believe I'm going to be a father!"

Chapter Twenty

James's graduation was a time of great healing for Jennifer. When she heard his testimony and the effect it had on the others at the Teen Challenge Center it moved her beyond what she expected. She believed him, when he told them of his conversion and what God had done in his life. The families of the other men had tears in their eyes when he spoke of the love of God and how He could change them, if He could change him. He talked of his past and how he would manipulate first his family and then he turned to manipulating women to get them into his bed. He talked about the abuse of drugs and alcohol and how it could ruin their lives and bring consequences far more than they could imagine. He spoke in a quiet voice but his emotion penetrated those who were listening.

Tears slid down Jennifer's face when he spoke. He couldn't look at her because he was afraid he would break down. But his words were for her ears. Forgiveness poured from her eyes and a new love began to seep into her heart. God was showing her His precious love for James. When he spoke of forgiveness and love, her baby leapt in her stomach. She could feel her precious daughter move in a way she had never felt before. She stroked her gently and told her that was her daddy talking. She could feel the Holy Spirit move all over the room captivating the hearts around her. She marveled at the thought.

Jason and Sondra were also moved by his testimony. They had heard it before but a new passion was emanating from him. Sondra smiled at how wonderful the grace of God was. In the corner of her eye, she watched Jennifer's reaction to what James was saying and couldn't help but see a new love in her eyes for him. She didn't know what it meant but she was sure that Jennifer was feeling something fresh and new for her brother-in-law. She sighed, wondering what would come of all this.

Jason stood up and clapped the loudest when James was finished. He asked if he could say a few words and Bill nodded his head yes.

"Today, God is writing a new chapter in my brother's life. I cannot tell you how much God has changed his life. I feel like I am listening to a stranger but I assure you it is the same James he was telling you about. I am so glad that God has shown us how 'He takes away the old and brings forth the new' when we surrender to Him. Well, today I am seeing a new man. I am so proud of you, James. I can hardly wait to see where God takes you in the future. I love you dearly, brother." He went over and gave James a big bear hug. Everyone clapped and cheered for them. The atmosphere turned from somber to jubilant.

They all had drinks and snacks while James went upstairs to his room to say goodbye to his roomies and to the time he spent there praying and crying out to God. His roommates greeted him there and slapped him on the back and told him how much they were going to miss him. Jonathan especially was happy and yet sad to see him depart.

"I'm going to miss you, James. You have been more than a brother to me these last seven months. I don't know what we are going to do without your ugly face around here," he joked as he hugged him. "Thanks for everything. I will never forget you."

"This is not goodbye, Jonathan. It's only 'I'll see you later.'" He spoke with emotion. When you get out of here I hope you will come and see me."

"I wouldn't miss it for anything. I hear you're going to be a father. Now that is scary." He laughed again. "Congratulations, brother. I know you will be a great father. Are you going to marry her?"

"I don't know, Jonathan. I know I should but I can't tell you if she would even have me. I would 'covet' your prayers though. I'm still in shock and I still have a lot to learn and, I hate to admit it, but I'm a little afraid of leaving this place. It's become my safe haven. What if I go back to my old ways?"

"James, only prayer and the grace of God can keep our past in the past. You have a new future to write so I say to you 'go and write it.' Your slate is clean. You are an amazing man of God and we are all honored to have known you. You will be just fine. Remember what you have learned here and make us all proud." He slapped him on the back again. "Now get out of here," he laughed.

"I'll be back for your graduation." He walked reluctantly out of the room not looking behind him. He was looking ahead.

James came home that day and he began to write a new chapter in his life. He wrote in his journal every day to keep himself on the straight and narrow. Roberta was thrilled by his help in the kitchen. At the center he cooked most of the meals and he had learned to be very creative with what little they had. He worked hard in the fields with the ranch hands. He asked to pray before meals and start up a Bible Study for the hands living at Willow Oaks. It was almost too good to be true. For Sondra and Jason, it was like having a breath of fresh air in the house. They wondered deep in their hearts how long it would last.

~

Tommy was unusually happy as he sauntered in two weeks before Valentine's Day. He kissed Cassie with a deep longing that morning. He sat her down on his knee and whispered in her ear.

"I have a present for you my darling."

Cassie giggled and wondered what he had up his sleeve. "Tell me, fair prince, what is it that you have."

"How would you like to be my wife on Valentine's Day?"

"What did you just say?" she asked, startled and jumped off his knee as if he had burned her.

"How would you like to marry me on Valentine's Day?" he repeated, a little worried that she wasn't jumping for joy.

"I heard what you said but I can't believe you said it!"

"What are you talking about, Cassie?" He stood up and tried to put his arms around her. "I thought you wanted to marry me. I thought you would be delighted. Jason and I have set the whole thing up."

"You spoke to Jason before you even consulted me?" She stomped her foot. "This is our wedding, Tommy, and I wanted to plan it. With the babies coming soon I won't have time to plan our wedding." She fussed and paced the floor. "How could you be so inconsiderate?"

Tommy rubbed his chin in frustration.

"I thought you would be delighted. You won't have to do a thing. Just show up and say 'I do'." He smiled as he teased her.

"But I want to plan our wedding, Tommy. I have dreamed about it for the last year. So many things came up that interfered with our plans — for instance Sondra's wedding, the babies, and the worry over James. I can't put my mind around 'us.'"

"Isn't it about time you put 'us' first? You can plan the wedding, Cassie. No one wants to take that from you. I can hardly wait to hold you in my arms, not just for a few hours but for a whole night and then a whole lifetime. You are my love, my light, my day. I dream about you at night, Cassie, and I hate to say it, but my body longs to be one with yours. Can you understand that? I love you." He brought her close and stroked her hair and tenderly put his lips on hers.

Cassie was mesmerized by his words and his actions.

"Do you think it's even possible?"

"Yes Cassie, it's time for you and me. I can't wait anymore and I won't wait. I need you to say yes, darling." She looked at him and paused taking a deep breath.

"Okay, Valentine's Day it is." She smiled with a quirky smile. "Can you wait that long?"

He pulled her in his arms and twirled her around happily.

"What's all the commotion?" A voice came from the kitchen.

"We're getting married on Valentine's Day. Can you believe it?" Cassie answered excitedly with flushed cheeks.

During the flurry of activity in making plans for the wedding Jason too had made plans for adopting Maria. They had many discussions on the idea of adopting her and they were both on the same page. Sondra couldn't have been happier.

He and Sondra agreed that they would bring her into their home while they waited for the adoption papers. She had been part of their Christmas celebration and now she would be a flower girl for Cassie's wedding. Pastor Jose assured them that the paperwork was only a formality and that they could first become foster parents to little Maria. She was excited about becoming part of their family.

She arrived at Willow Oaks on a Saturday morning. Pastor Jose brought her to the house with a small suitcase in her hand. Her large brown eyes had tears in them when Sondra opened the door and held out her arms. She put down her little suitcase and ran into her arms. Sondra hugged her and kissed her with tears running down her cheeks.

"I'm so happy you have come, darling. Welcome to your new home," she managed to whisper to her.

"Are you going to be my mommy and daddy?" She looked at them with huge brown eyes.

"Yes, sweetheart, we are hoping we will be your new mommy and daddy. Would you like that?" She smiled and looked into her beautiful face.

"Oh yes, please," she spoke politely.

Sondra just hugged her again and lifted her up and carried her into the house. Jason took her from Sondra and gave her a look. "You shouldn't be lifting her. Let me do the lifting, okay?" Sondra shook her head yes.

"Hello, Maria. Would you like to come and see your new bedroom?"

"Oh, yes I would." She smiled and hugged Jason with all her strength.

"Let's go and meet everyone." He put her on the ground and took her hand and showed her around the house.

They had redecorated one of the rooms next to James's bedroom into a little girl's dream room. The furniture was white with a gold trim. Her favorite color was purple so all the trimmings were that rich deep purple. The bedspread and the curtains came to life with the vibrant color. Toys and stuffed animals graced the shelves and topped the bed. The walls were freshly painted in a light purple with white trim. Maria's eyes took in everything the room had to offer. She was so excited that she screamed in delight. She ran and jumped on the fluffy down covered bedspread. Sondra laughed at her enthusiasm.

"Thank you, Miss Sondra. I love it." She hugged Sondra again. "Can I really stay here with you in this bedroom?"

"All this belongs to you, Maria. We want you to be part of our family." Sondra knelt down and faced her. "Would you like to be part of our family? You do know that little Jacob will be coming into the world soon?" She shook her head yes. "Is that okay with you?"

James had come out of his room to watch this cute little girl become part of their family. He shook his head and marveled at how wonderful God was. He felt that Maria was the most blessed little girl to be a part of his brother's and Sondra's lives. They would be wonderful parents.

He thought about his unborn little girl. Would he be as good a father as Jason? He wondered if he would be given a chance. He had been begging God to give him an answer on what he should do concerning Jennifer. He

185

wanted to do the right thing and marry her but he wasn't sure that was the best thing for her. She deserved more than he could give her. She needed a man who truly loved her. He wasn't sure he could be that man.

He loved her but not the way she needed to be loved. He wanted to marry her out of obligation to their unborn child and he argued with himself that he could learn to love her, but that wouldn't be fair to her. In the end, he decided he would wait on God for the answer. Many were praying for him but the wait was weighing heavily on him.

Little did he know that his wait was right around the corner!

Chapter Twenty-One

Cassie's beautiful bridal dress hung on a hanger outside her closet. She looked at it each night before she went to bed. Tonight, she sighed as she imagined — this time tomorrow — she would become Mrs. Thomas James O'Connor. Excitement flowed through her veins at the anticipation of fully becoming his wife. Cassie loved him with all her heart.

He was kind, loving, and sometimes a little demanding but sincere in his love for her. He could be overly protective but she enjoyed how he put her before anything else in his life. He made her feel needed and he treasured her like his princess.

She prayed that night that she would become the wife that Tommy needed. She would support him and help him reach the highest goals in his life. He had plans to make Parker Valley the most prosperous organic beef ranch in the country. Already, he had put into effect his ideas and with the approval of Sondra, he worked hard to achieve his objectives. She would be the sun in his shine and, if anyone came between them, she would become a woman to be reckoned with. Tommy would have his hands full.

She was tiny but she was strong. She cooked, cleaned and ruled the homestead with an iron fist. No one would dare swear in front of her or utter crude jokes around the table or they would feel her steely stare and her fiery wrath. The ranch hands respected her for her beliefs and rarely went against her policies. They admired her for her hard work and delicious food. She mothered them by patching up their wounds and nursing them when they were sick. They, in return, would protect her with their lives. She welcomed them into her family and treated them like gold. It gave them a sense of pride to be a part of a family away from their own families.

The wedding would be a small family affair, with only a few outside guests. Pastor Jose would officiate over their vows in the church and they would attend a reception at Willow Oaks afterwards.

Cassie woke up with a start. Jennifer was sitting on her bed smiling with a tray of food.

"Good morning, Cassie. You are getting married today. Can you believe it? I wanted to be the first to wake you on the last day of being a single woman." She laughed.

"Well, you certainly are in a good mood." She sat up and hugged her sister and took the tray from her. Steaming coffee was the first on her taste list.

"I have made breakfast for everyone this morning so you can relax in bed and get in the 'bridal mode'. You look wonderful this morning." She got up and lifted up her wedding dress. "You are going to look so beautiful, Cassie."

Cassie watched her sister dance around the room with her bridal gown in her hand.

"Are you okay about me getting married, Jennifer? Tommy will be living here and I hope it doesn't put a damper on you."

"Oh Cassie, I am just so happy for you. You know that I love Tommy. I know he doesn't always approve of me but I will show him how wonderful I am. Are you okay with me being here?"

"This is your home, Jennifer. You stay here as long as you want. Someday, you will be married and live with your spouse. I think that will be very soon. You are quite a catch."

Jennifer pranced around with her pregnant stomach sticking out and laughed. "Yeah, I'm quite a catch alright. You get two for the price of one!"

"If it wasn't for your sense of humor, I don't know what we would do."

"What's all the commotion about?" a sleepy voice asked from the doorway.

"Claira, why don't you come on in? We are having a party." She sat on the bed and took a piece of toast from her tray and started eating.

"Where's my coffee?" she complained jokingly.

Jennifer jumped up and said, "I'll be right back."

That gave Claira and Cassie time to chat.

"Are you okay with me getting married to Tommy and living here in the house? I hope it won't be inconvenient for you."

"Oh Cassie, all I want is your happiness. We all love Tommy. He has been a fixture here for almost a year now. Besides, I spend most of my time at the shop. I'm sorry I haven't been around to help you with your wedding. My clients have been insistent about getting their Valentine's gowns on time. It seems like I have outfitted the entire country and western crowd all over Texas. It is so exciting. I am now getting orders from Hollywood. I hope I can keep up with it. I need a good rest. I'm not working all this week. The shop is closed. I finished all the gowns two days ago and shipped them out. My staff deserves a week off after all the hustle and bustle." She sighed happily.

"Well you're making lots of money, my dear. I do hope they have paid you well."

"Oh, yes. They have certainly made it worth my while. I can't believe how well things have been going. Do you like the dress I made for you, Cassie? It is a special design. No one in the world will have a wedding dress like you do."

"I absolutely love it, Claira. Thank you so much. You are the best." She hugged her sister.

"Well I hope you can take some more surprises." She looked mysterious. "I'll be right back."

Cassie waited as Jennifer brought in Claira's coffee.

"Where did she go?"

"She is bringing in a surprise." She giggled like a school girl. "I wonder what it is."

Claira came in with a handful of dresses for Cassie to try on.

"The girls at the shop wanted you to have these. They were designed especially with you in mind."

She deposited the clothes on the bed. They ranged from a beautiful sequin dress of light green, blue and gold. It was beautiful. It would show off her beautiful shoulders and tiny waist. Cassie's mouth hung open as she surveyed the outfits fit for a princess. There were nightgowns and housecoats, pant suits, and skirts with exquisite blouses.

"Oh Claira, they are magnificent. Thank you so much. I will be the belle of the ball." Tears formed in her eyes. "How can I ever repay you?"

"Just wear them in style and be sure to tell people where you got them." She laughed as she hugged her sister.

She got up and tried them all on excitedly. They fit like a glove. She would look like royalty in them. They spent the rest of the day getting ready for the evening activities. They all had their hair done and makeup brushed on. By five o'clock they were ready for the festivities.

They met the rest of the family at the church sharp at one o'clock. The church decorated in elegant wedding fashion. Lights twinkled all over the sanctuary. They had brought in trees and beautiful flowers graced the front and back of the church. Excitement permeated everywhere. There was going to be a wedding.

Cassie looked elegant in her full length wedding gown. Her petite size graced the gown with perfection. It was strapless with a lace overview. Tiny folds rippled softly from her waistline to the floor. When she moved, it swished with her movements. She wore a tiara laced with tiny crystals that shimmered in the twinkling light. Her veil only covered her face but fell gently to the end of her gown in the back. Her tiny white shoes were barely visible through her wedding dress.

Claira, her maid of honor, wore a burgundy short sleeveless dress with a silver laced belt. The other sisters wore the same colored burgundy dresses only in a maternity style. They wore their hair up and off their shoulders. They all painted a lovely picture.

Jason had hired a harpist and three violinists. The music gave sophistication to the service. As the guests were seated, they waited in anticipation for the ceremony to begin.

Tommy waited anxiously at the front of the sanctuary for his bride to walk down the aisle. Beads of sweat started to form on his forehead. Jason smiled and patted him on the back and told him to relax. It would soon be over.

Pastor Jose entered through the door at the front of the church and nodded to Claira to begin. The violinists began to play and Sondra started down the aisle. She carried one white rose in her hands, with baby's-breath mixed in. She smiled as she caught the eye of her handsome husband in his tux. He smiled in return as he admired his bride of nearly seven months. Jennifer came next nervously clutching her rose. After her, little Maria entered the sanctuary carrying a basket of white rose petals. Her tiny hands dutifully laid white petals on the white runner as she walked down the aisle. Claira, her maid of honor, walked in next. Everyone smiled in delight at her intense look. She looked beautiful in her gown. The doors closed after her. When she reached the front of the sanctuary, Sondra smiled at her and they stood facing the front together, waiting for Cassie to appear.

As the music changed, the door opened and Cassie appeared in all her splendor. Manuel, their long time stable hand and longtime friend, walked her down the aisle. He was a second father to all the girls growing up. He chastised them when they needed a firm hand and rewarded them with praise when they were successful. After their parent's sudden death, he and his wife stepped in to help and guide them. They were dearly loved. He proudly walked Cassie down the aisle to meet her bridegroom. He lifted her veil and kissed her cheek, with a tear running down his own.

The ceremony was beautiful. Pastor Jose did a wonderful job of highlighting their lives together with a promise that God would guide them through the trials and tribulations that life would bring. A tearful Cassie said her vows with Tommy looking on. His eyes held a deep tenderness towards the woman he was marrying. She would become his soul mate to love, honor, and cherish. He took it very seriously. When they kissed, the spectators clapped vigorously. They made a striking couple.

Sondra gazed into Jason's eyes during the ceremony, remembering her own wedding that seemed like only yesterday. She smiled as Cassie's and Tommy's lips locked together. They were one in the Spirit.

As they left the sanctuary, she took Jason's' hand and kissed it. He smiled back with a question look in his eyes.

She whispered in his ear, "I love you, Jason Nelson." He winked back. He then picked up Maria and carried her out.

"You were wonderful, Maria. And you looked beautiful in your new dress." Maria giggled in delight.

Cassie and Tommy greeted every person as they left the sanctuary. Everyone then rode back to Willow Oaks together for the reception.

Chapter Twenty-Two

Jennifer agreed with everyone that this was the best Valentine's Day they ever had. Weddings had a habit of giving one the sense of a fairytale.

When they entered the front door of Willow Oaks they were greeted with a delightful entourage of caterers. Delicate appetizers were made available by an efficient staff hired by Roberta. There was champagne, nonalcoholic for the children, and spiced cider for the adults. The festive atmosphere filtered throughout the ranch. The ranch hands and their families, along with close neighbors, had all been invited to share the happy occasion with Cassie and Tommy.

An elegant buffet dinner was served at three o'clock and everyone helped themselves to the feast of roast beef, chicken and shrimp dishes. There was a children's corner where they could help themselves to chicken fingers and french-fries. No one was left out of the celebration of marriage.

James found Jennifer sitting in a corner chatting with one of the children.

"Hello, Jennifer." He approached her shyly.

"Hello, James. Wasn't it a wonderful wedding?" She stared up at him.

"It was beautiful. I was so proud of Cassie and Tommy. They finally decided to get married and start their lives together. In a sense, I'm a little jealous of their special love they share together," he said.

Jennifer just looked at him wondering why he would think of such a thing. Did he want to settle down and get married? Her heart started to race. She held her breath while he continued to speak.

"It's a love that is almost impossible to find in this day and age. Jason and Sondra too have this quality about their marriage. Strange isn't it? God has really blessed them, hasn't He?"

It was at that moment that Andrew came up to Jennifer and looked at James with his steel gray eyes.

"Is everything okay Jennifer?" He looked James in the eye.

"Yes, Andrew. Have you met Jason's brother, James, yet?" Her attitude changed as soon as he appeared. She stood up. "James, this is Andrew. Andrew, this is James, Jason's brother." Andrew shook his hand, his eyes not leaving his. He didn't say a word.

"It's nice to meet you. Are you a relation to Jennifer?" James asked him, a little shaken by his intense look.

He shook his head without saying a word.

"Will you be okay?" He looked at Jennifer with dark eyes.

Jennifer laughed and punched his shoulder. "Yes, Andrew. I'll be fine."

James noticed the difference in her attitude when she spoke to Andrew. She became coy and relaxed, as if they had a bond together. He couldn't help but feel a little jealous of their candid rapport. 'Who was this guy?' he thought to himself. 'What is he to Jennifer?'

James watched him walk away without looking back.

"Who was that guy?" His voice was a little defensive.

"Why? Are you jealous? Am I not allowed to have relationships around here?" She stared at him a little angry that he would take such an offense. "It's not like you've been around lately." She stomped off in the direction of the buffet table.

"What did I say wrong?" He watched her leave.

"Absolutely nothing! That's the problem," she yelled back.

James shook his head not understanding what just went down. 'Women are hard to understand,' he thought as he went to find Jason.

Jennifer was upset that James had been home for over two weeks and had not contacted her at all. She felt rejected and alone. She didn't know what she had hoped for but it wasn't to be ignored.

She wasn't sure of her feelings for James and she was a little sensitive. 'How dare he just come up upon me and pretend that everything was cool?' she thought, as a fresh batch of tears welled up.

Just at that moment, Claira came up to her and put her arm around her.

"Is everything okay, little sister?" She joked as she noticed a few tears in her eyes. "I saw you talking to James. Did he say something to upset you, sweetheart?"

Jennifer rubbed her eyes embarrassed that she would notice. "I don't know what comes over me when he is around. He makes me crazy. My heart speeds up and I get tongue tied."

"Could it be that you are in love with him, honey?"

Jennifer just looked at her and shook her head. "I don't know. How does anyone know?"

"I don't know, sweetheart. You just know. And, don't worry. You will know." She put her arm around her shoulder and they both went to get some food.

Everyone woke that next morning a little tired but satisfied that Cassie's wedding was perfect. The bride and groom were sleeping at Willow Oaks in their lovely guest room. Sondra had it redecorated by a decorator from Dallas and it was fit to be the Honeymoon Suite. The furniture was cherry wood with a huge four poster king-size bed. The massive furniture fit perfectly in the oversized room.

There was an on suite bathroom that featured a Jacuzzi tub and full size shower, and a separate room for the toilet and bidet. Downy soft white towels hung on the holders and were draped over the bathtub. Candles graced the countertop and around the Jacuzzi. Any accessory that was needed was stuffed in the white laced basket on the gray-granite counter.

The decorator took special care in the bedding. The bed was decked out in white sheets with a beautiful white silk down comforter gracing its surface. Six fluffy pillows topped it off making the bed look cozy and inviting. Sondra wanted to make sure that Cassie and Tommy would be comfortable and their night would be memorable.

Roberta knocked on their door at eight thirty that morning with a beautiful tray full of all their favorite breakfast foods. There was a silver tea and coffee set, with white china cups and plates. A basket of homemade muffins and a plate full of bacon and scrambled eggs was the fare for the day. She put the tray inside the room on the coffee table. She smiled at the couple whose eyes were droopy from sleep.

"Good morning, you love birds. I thought you might like to have your breakfast in bed instead of downstairs. You two just take your time. We will see you when you come down stairs. Don't be too long though. Little Maria is chomping at the bit to see you. She still has wedding fever." She laughed and closed the door behind her.

Tommy and Cassie looked at each other with a twinkle in their eyes and laughed with her.

"Good morning, darling," Tommy said to Cassie as he kissed her gently on the lips.

"Good morning." She shyly kissed him back. They got up and enjoyed their first breakfast together as husband and wife.

~

Jennifer woke up that morning with a start. Her heart was racing and her breathing became shallow.

She had dreamt she was walking down the aisle so pregnant that she looked like she was carrying a basketball. She was wearing a red wedding gown with white slippers and a white veil covered her head. As she walked down the aisle she saw a man at the altar. He was wearing a white tuxedo and had on a black top hat. She couldn't see his face, but as she got a little closer another man came out from the pews and tapped her on the shoulder. He too, was wearing a white tux, but had on a black Stetson Hat. She was confused when he put out his arm to walk her down. When the man at the front turned to face her he was faceless. She frantically turned to the gentleman that was walking with her and he too was faceless.

Jennifer mulled over her dream and wondered what it meant. 'Maybe I'm going crazy,' she thought to herself. 'Maybe Sondra can interpret my dream.'

Jennifer thought about last night and wondered why her emotions were so vulnerable when James was around. She felt it could have been pregnancy jitters but she was determined to confront him and get her feelings out in the open. 'But, not today,' she said to herself as she brushed her teeth. She would put aside all her worries and enjoy the day. Today was going to be a special day.

It was Maria's birthday and they were all going to celebrate it at Willow Oaks tonight. It was her first birthday with a real family. Sondra spent the last week buying presents for her.

When it came time, she opened toys and books of every nature. Sondra and Jason showered her with new dresses and pants and riding clothes. Her big surprise came later when everyone went out to the barn to show her the new pony that Sondra and Jason had bought for her. He was a honey colored Shetland pony that was so tiny; Maria could reach up and touch his long mane. She jumped up and down and couldn't believe that she had her own horse.

Jason squatted on his heels and bent down and looked her in the eyes.

"I don't want you riding him alone okay? I want you to make sure someone is there with you at all times or you will have to deal with me. Is that understood?" He looked at her seriously.

"Yes, Mr. Jason. I won't ride him alone. I promise."

"Good girl. Now why don't you jump on his back and I will help you go for a ride? Would you like that?"

She squealed again as he lifted her on her pony's back. They walked around the yard together. She couldn't have been happier. Sondra watched the two of them and grinned from ear to ear. One of the concerns they had was that she was too young to ride a horse.

Sondra complained that she was only two years old when she received her first horse. And it wasn't a pony. She felt Jason was being overly protective about the subject. He thought because she had not been around horses all her life that it would be better to let her start out with something smaller. He worried that Maria wouldn't respect the horses as she should, because of her lack of experience. Sondra soon gave in and it appeared Jason was right. She loved the pony.

After all her presents were opened, and laughter filled the room, they all sat down for a quiet dinner. Cassie and Tommy went back to their room and everyone smiled to themselves. The two love birds needed to have some time alone.

Jennifer was so moved by what Jason and Sondra had done with Maria that she started volunteering at the orphanage two days a week. She loved the children and they loved her. She thought this would give her a chance to find out what it would be like to be a mother. Every time she went to the center, the children wanted to touch her stomach. She was growing in girth every day. She was fast realizing that the birth of her child would be soon. She had six weeks to go. During the time of her pregnancy, she kept her regular meetings with Carol Briggs. They discussed everything from the loss of her parents to her upcoming motherhood. Jennifer was being grounded in truth and her faith was blossoming.

Her sessions one day began when Carol started talking about her feelings about her future.

"So, Jennifer, when you go home this week I want you to pray about what you think God has planned for your future. What are your short term goals and your long term goals? What do you envision your life will be like in a one year period, and what your life will look like in ten years' time? It doesn't have to be elaborate, but I want you to be realistic and honest. Can you do that for me for our next visit?" She handed her a chart and a notebook.

"I'm not quite sure what you mean. Do I put down what I dream my life will be like or what I know of today?"

"Jennifer, I want you to dream. What are your aspirations and ideas you thought life would be like when you were a child? What did you say when people asked you 'when you grow up what do you want to be?' Some children dreamt of being a teacher, an astronaut or a fireman. What did you dream about?

Don't make it too difficult. Just dream, okay? But spend some time in prayer before you answer."

Jennifer sat in thought as Carol continued.

"Then after you have done that, I want you to write down your gifting's." She handed her a questionnaire to fill in. "This will help guide you through the process. Let's see if it adds up to your dreams and visions. God has gifted each one of us with special talents. I want to know if you know what your talents are. I believe you have many. You are using some and probably are unaware of others. It will be a good exercise for you to go through. It opens our eyes to the future."

"I will do my best," she said.

~

It was harder and harder for Sondra to get around the closer she got to her delivery date. Her due date was around the same time as Jennifer's, but the baby seemed to be much bigger.

"Your son is complaining an awful lot lately," she grumbled to Jason one morning. "He hardly let me sleep at all last night. I hope this isn't a precursor to when he is born."

"He is certainly getting to be a big boy." Jason absently put his hand on her abdomen.

She slapped it away playfully. "Are you saying I'm getting too fat?"

"No darling, don't be so sensitive. All I'm saying is that our son will be a healthy good sized boy. And he will get much bigger during your last few weeks."

She groaned inwardly. "I don't know if I can handle that, Jason. I think he is big enough."

Just at that moment, a pitter patter of little feet came running down the hallway and barged into the room squealing in delight. James was chasing her and pretending to be a monster. She jumped up on the bed and settled between them.

"Save me, mommy," she said, innocently hiding behind Sondra hugging her.

Sondra looked at Maria and gulped. It was the first time she had called her mommy. It took Sondra by surprise and she looked at Jason with tears in her eyes. He smiled at her and grabbed Maria and playfully tickled her.

"I won't let the monster get you. I will protect you." He jumped up and started to wrestle with James. They all laughed until tears rolled down Maria's cheeks. Her laugh was contagious.

"Oh daddy, you are the best monster killer in the world," she said innocently, hugging him.

Jason looked back at Sondra and gave her a brilliant smile. It was at that moment that they truly felt like Maria was part of their family.

Chapter Twenty-Three

James's Bible Study for the ranch hands was going well. He was convinced that it would make a difference in their lives. The first meeting was more successful than he could imagine. He wondered if the men wanted to give him the benefit of the doubt because of the change they noticed in him. When he came back from the center, he worked harder and longer than anyone else. He felt he had to prove himself to the other hands. Every one of the ranch hands and his brother Jason showed up at his meeting except Andrew.

James would address that issue another day. He wondered what his problem was. Ever since Cassie's wedding, Andrew had kept a close eye on him. James could feel him watching his every move. Now and then, he could see a spark of approval in his gaze, but he never said a word.

James poured his heart into his first Bible Study on Acts. His fiery account of the disciples being filled with the Holy Spirit had them all mesmerized. His charismatic ability captured their hearts and James was blown away by their response. He was genuinely surprised by their knowledge of the Bible and was encouraged to continue the weekly study. Jason gave his nod of approval after the men had left.

"Good job, James. The men seem to be captivated by your rendition of the disciples. You're very good at what you do, brother, and I would like to see this continue as much as possible. Are you up for it?"

"It's in my blood Jason. I only want to please God. When I talk about the Word of God my heart starts pumping and I get so excited." They sat down together and James continued to seek his counsel.

"What's up with Andrew?"

"Why? What has he done to discourage you?" he asked.

"It's nothing that I know of but I get the strange feeling that he is watching me and judging me. I know he disapproves of me and my actions. I don't know if he will ever understand what I have been through the last seven months. He has probably heard about what happened with Jennifer and me. In fact, he seems very protective of her. What is that all about?"

Jason looked at his brother seriously. "Andrew and Jennifer have been through a lot in the last four or five months too. You probably haven't heard about what Jennifer has been through. It hasn't been all fun and games for her, James. Why don't you sit down and talk to her about it? She has a lot to tell you." He got up and shook his hand and thanked him for the Bible Study, and went back to the house.

James sat alone in the room and started to pray. He prayed for guidance and patience as he walked out his salvation. He thanked God for giving him the words to speak and a heart to express them.

~

The next day, James called over to Parker Valley and made arrangements to see Jennifer. She was a little hesitant but agreed to see him that afternoon.

He arrived with his hat in his hand. "Hello, James." Jennifer greeted him and showed him into the living room. She had blossomed into a beautiful woman who was carrying his baby. His heart flew into his throat. He gulped and was humbled by her gentle demeanor.

"You look great, Jennifer. How are you feeling?" His eyes did not leave hers.

"A lot better thank you. But I am looking forward to losing this basketball I'm carrying."

"You couldn't look better in my eyes." He shifted in his chair and shifted his eyes to the floor, trying to gain control again. "I was talking to Jason last night and he mentioned that you had been through a rough time the last four or five months. Would you consider talking to me about it?"

She looked at him with a question in her eyes. "What do you want to know? I have gotten over a lot of my anger, disappointment, and delusion of why God would allow me to be raped, pregnant, and alone. What else would you like to know about what I've gone through?" She smiled but it didn't reach her eyes.

208

James bent his head and said a little prayer. "I can understand that you would be hurt and upset with all you have been through. It is my fault that you have had to go through this, Jennifer. I am so truly sorry." He gulped and continued.

"If I could change it all, I would in a heartbeat. I was selfish, self-centered, egotistical, arrogant and proud. I am ashamed to have taken part in what I did to you. I will spend the rest of my life regretting my actions." He stopped and bent over and took her hand.

"One blessing that has come from this tragedy is that a new life will come into this world. God has given us a special gift, Jennifer. I have learned that God takes something that was meant for evil and turns it into something for His glory. She may have been conceived out of deceit but she was made in the image of God, before the foundation of the world. She will be a child of the King and she will have the most wonderful mother in the whole world. Her biological father will try not to be the idiot he started out to be." He smiled sadly.

Jennifer stared at him wondering if he was sincere. She had seen a huge difference in his life since coming home from the Teen Challenge Center. At first, she wanted him to suffer for what he put her through, but now she was happy that he was healed and whole. Everyone needed that. She was content that he would be happy and a good father to her little girl.

"Jennifer, I have a great desire to go to seminary. To learn all I can about who God is and what my purpose in life is. I can start a class the end of April." He paused and looked into her eyes. "I want you to go with me. I want you to marry me and let me take care of you for the rest of your life and our baby's life. I want to have lots of children with you." He laughed getting caught up in the excitement.

"Ever since I met you, I have been captivated by you. I think I have been a little afraid of my feelings towards you. I love you Jennifer. Will you consider being part of my present and future?" He looked deep into her eyes.

Jennifer just stared at him with her mouth open. She was not expecting him to ask her to marry him. She coughed slightly.

"Why James, this is such a surprise. I didn't expect this at all. I don't know what to say." She stood up and walked around the room. "Why would you want to marry me? Is it because I am having your baby?" She was getting a little agitated. The last thing she wanted was for him to feel sorry for her.

"No Jennifer, I didn't even know myself what I was going to say to you. When I looked at you I realized how much in love with you I am. You have captivated my heart. The baby is just a plus for me, and perhaps, because of her, it will be 'hurry up mode.' God works in mysterious ways."

She just stared at him, surprise still written all over her face.

"I have to think about this." She paced the room. "I don't know, James. I don't want to marry you because of our baby, but I am not sure that I am in love with you the same way you are in love with me."

James did not let that bother him. He expected that she would say that. They hadn't had a chance to get to know each other.

"Why don't you think about it and, tonight, let me take you to dinner. We could talk and get to know one another. Does that sound fair?" She nodded yes and he took her hand and turned it over and kissed it. "I will wait for as long as it takes to convince you of my love for you, Jennifer. God has changed my heart and I will wait for Him to change yours." He left the house.

Jennifer sat down on the couch, shocked about what just happened. "Dear God, show me what to do," she cried out in a soft voice. The next thing she knew, Cassie was sitting beside her, holding her hand.

"Oh Cassie, James was just here. He has asked me to marry him. What shall I do? I am so confused." She said tears running down her face as he hugged her sister.

"I heard, Jennifer. I was in the other room. I wanted to make sure you were okay, so I was listening a little. I hope you don't mind." She smiled as she hugged her sister back. "What do you think?"

"That's the same question I was going to ask you, Cassie. I am a little scared. What should I do?"

"Do you love him, Jennifer?"

"I don't know. I did a little before this all happened. He has always been an enigma to me. He was flirty, forward and there was something a little wild about him that attracted me to him. But, now that he has changed so much, I see a perfect gentleman, one who loves the

Lord and would do anything to please Him. I am definitely attracted to that side of him. I would be marrying someone I was equally yoked with. But I can't help but think this marriage proposal came from guilt."

Cassie just nodded, deep in thought. "He does want to further his education which is good. I don't know how he will support you and the baby while he does that. Probably it would be a stipend from Jason. Perhaps you could go to school at the same time and put the baby in day care. Would you consider that?"

"Cassie, you are forgetting that he has asked me to marry him. That is a big commitment," she stated.

"Jennifer, I think in a small way you are very much in love with James. I can see it in your eyes. But you are the one that has to live with him." She smiled at her shocked look.

"I have to think about this." She paced the room. "Getting to know him better is good too. I have at least another six weeks before the baby is born. That gives me lots of time." She looked at her sister and cried out.

"Cassie, I don't want a husband out of guilt. I want a man who will love me for who I am. I have to make sure it is not out of pity or guilt that he wants to marry me. Do you think I am being foolish? Do you think that's crazy?" she ranted on.

Cassie just looked on and smiled at her sister. 'She is definitely in love,' she thought to herself. 'God help both of them.'

Chapter Twenty-Four

James and Jennifer went to dinner that night and talked the whole time. They shared their thoughts and desires together for the first time. Jennifer found it hard to share her feelings at first but she soon found him easy to talk to. He shared his life challenges and she shared her fears and trials she faced.

He kissed her goodnight for the first time since their last encounter. He was gentle and warm, which melted Jennifer's heart. At first she thought she would be repulsed but it was just the opposite. She smiled at him and said goodnight. When she closed the door, she leaned against it and nearly collapsed. "Dear God, he makes me crazy," she said out loud.

They met during the day and every night for a week. Finally, James asked her the question she was dreading.

"Have you made a decision yet? Are you ready to marry this crazy guy, who is crazy about you?

She looked at him seriously and took a deep breath and confessed. "I am not sure whether I'm willing to commit to marriage yet. I need more time to get to know you. I hope you understand, James. It's not that I am saying 'no.' I'm just saying maybe."

He nodded his head in agreement. "I will take that as an encouragement to continue seeing you. Would that be okay?"

"I like being with you, James. You make me laugh." She punched his arm in jest.

He snuggled next to her and brought up another question.

"So, tell me what your relationship is with Andrew."

She looked at him and smiled inwardly. "What relationship are you talking about?"

"It's the way he looks at you. He seems to be protecting you in some say. He is very possessive when it comes to you, Jennifer. That is as plain as the eye can see."

"Are you jealous?"

"That depends on the relationship you have with him."

She laughed at his seriousness. "You are jealous!"

He sat back on the sofa trying, not to look miffed. "It's not that I am jealous. It's that I am curious about the connection the two of you have. If you are in love with someone else, Jennifer, you need to tell me. If you are seeing me and secretly in love with another man, then yes I would be jealous, and that is not a godly trait."

"Okay, I will tell you," she said, reluctant to express her feeling that even she wasn't sure of. "Jason was threatened about two or three months ago. They said they would harm me if he didn't stop the proceedings of some land deal. He put Andrew on the case as my body guard." She began to explain Andrew's character and his background with the Navy Seals and what transpired with the kidnapping. She left out the details of her rebellion and selfish childish behavior. She was not proud of the way she had acted.

"Well, then it's a good thing that he is around. I didn't realize that he was such an experienced and decorated service man. I know that he and Jason were best friends but I didn't realize to what extent. I would not want to be his adversary. And I can see how he would want to protect someone as sweet and innocent as you. No wonder he looked at me as such a scumbag."

"He looked at you that way?" she asked.

"If looks could kill, I would be dead. So tell me what your feelings are for this Andrew character. Sometimes maidens in distress tend to fall in love with their protectors. Did that happen to you?"

She laughed outright at his comment. "You really are crazy. As far as I know, I have no feelings for Andrew. I was just thankful that he was there. How he feels about me is another question. We have not spoken since he was pulled off the case."

That seemed to placate James as he settled down and began to talk to her about times when his brother would protect him.

They spent the rest of the day together sharing other experiences they had gone through. Their hearts were growing fonder for each other as they began to learn about their strengths and weaknesses.

~

On the other side of the valley, Andrew sat on his horse watching the men round up some of the lost cattle to take back to the ranch. It was cold and there were possible snow flurries in the forecast. They had to work fast before the weather settled in. The ground was hard and the land looked barren. The sky was clear with shadows of clouds in the distance. The cattle had little food this far out in the pastures so they would be taken to the area where they could survive the sudden cold winter. The harsh weather wouldn't last long but long enough to take a herd of cattle that wasn't protected.

As Andrew sat on his horse, his mind was transfixed thinking of Jennifer. He wasn't sure of his feelings towards her. One minute she was a young pregnant girl in need of protection and the next she was a woman with a strong passion for life. She breathed life to its fullest. She had been through a lot for a young girl of nineteen. He shook his head to dismiss his thoughts. 'What am I thinking? She is just a child.'

He had been offered a job with the State Department but he was content to work for Jason. He loved his job and was always ready to help out his friend. But an uneasy feeling crept in as he thought of Jennifer and James together. He was reluctant to attend his Bible Study. He wasn't sure whether it was out of spite or rebellion or that he just didn't like the young man for what he did to Jennifer and was having trouble forgiving him. He had to work out his state of mind when it came to thinking about the two of them together.

He rationalized his thoughts. First, he thought, James was the father of her baby. Second, it was good that they should be together, if not only for the baby's sake. He didn't have a right to come in and confuse the issue with his feelings towards Jennifer. He restructured in his head that she was too young for him in maturity and in age. He didn't know what he was thinking about. He ran his hand through his hair, as he held his hat in the other.

He took a deep breath and thought perhaps taking the State Department job would be a good thing. It would keep him away from Parker Valley and having to express his emotions. He prayed and asked God for a confirmation on the decision he should make. He would also seek counsel with Pastor Jose. Having made that decision, his heart was challenged to subdue his feelings for the young girl until he could talk to his elders. He and his horse joined the other men in hunting down the cattle and ushered them back to the ranch.

James, on the other hand, was pursuing Jennifer with an exuberance that he hadn't experienced in years. He felt like a kid at his first birthday party. His excitement was gathering strength one weekend when he went home for a visit. Jason had sent him on a quest back to Virginia to settle a few family matters. He was staying with his mother and father when they spoke to him about his thoughts and plans for the future, and marrying Jennifer. That was when he went to the family jeweler in Richmond.

They were excited about his attending Seminary School, and challenged him on being a father and a husband while taking classes.

"I really am excited about it, mom," James explained to his mother one evening. "I am hoping that Jennifer will go to school with me. We can put the baby in day care at the school and both of us can work around our classes. I have talked to Jennifer about it and I believe she is warming up to my plan."

"It will be a very challenging opportunity, dear, and it really sounds like you have thought out everything. Your dad and I will back you all the way. Four years is a long time but, if you two work hard, I know you will come out of school ready for whatever it is that God has planned for you. I'm proud of you, dear."

"Thanks, mom. And thank you also for your financial support. One day, I will pay you and dad and Jason back for all you have done for me. I am so sorry that I have squandered so much in the past. I hope you and dad will forgive me. I was a very selfish and a very disagreeable young man. God has opened my eyes in a big way."

Elaine smiled at her son and silently thanked God for the work He had done in his life. She knew that he would someday be the one to look out for in the Christian arena. He was a dynamic young man. She was very proud of him and how far he had come in the last eight months. 'God does amazing things when you pray,' she thought to herself.

"I want you to see what I have bought Jennifer." He was excited, as he took a black velvet case out of his pocket, with the logo of their favorite jewelry store. He showed his mother a beautiful two carat platinum gold solitaire ring. It sparkled when it hit the sunlight. Elaine gasped and showed her appreciation for her son's excellent taste. It was almost a perfect diamond. It had cost him a good chunk of his trust fund but she was worth it.

"Oh James, it is beautiful! I know that Jennifer will fall in love with it. I would love it too. Let's pray that she accepts it and the two of you start your lives together. I think it is wonderful. Do you have any idea when you might get married if she accepts your proposal?"

"Hopefully, we will get married as soon as we can put it together. I would like it to be before the baby is born and that is in at least five weeks. Hopefully it will be sooner than that. I really have fallen in love with her, mom. I pray and hope she accepts my proposal." He sighed nervously. "It's hard to believe that soon I will be a father and hopefully a husband. I have watched you and dad my whole life and I can only hope that I can emulate as good a marriage as you two."

His mother looked at him lovingly and smiled. "It takes a lot of prayer and a lot of forgiving but, most of all, a lot of communication. As long as you talk to each other about how you are feeling and your daily struggles and victories, you will be halfway there. When your father came home after working each day, we always spent at least a half an hour together talking about what happened that day. I always talked to him about the struggles in my life and he talked about his. We would hide nothing from each other. It bonded us together in a way that nothing else will. Our dependence on God to take the burden from us was another key factor in our marriage. But I think the most important balance in our marriage was forgiving each other. It will be a daily pastime in your life together as a couple. We all make mistakes and it takes a big person to realize it. Forgive yourself first and then forgive her." She sighed in remembrance of difficult times they had gone through.

"Most of all James, remember that what you are entering into is a covenant with God. It has nothing to do with love. Love is just the emotion that puts you together. It is a commitment to the Covenant that 'keeps' you together. Love and hate are related emotions. You will feel both but it will be God who binds the marriage together during the difficult times. And trust me there will be lots of difficult times. You are two different people, with two different ideas." When she saw the look of confusion on his face, she laughed.

"You will be just fine, son. Just pray and seek counsel when you need it."

"Thanks, mom, for your advice. It scares me a lot but I want to try and make it work."

"It has nothing to do with trying son. Either you decide to make it happen or you don't. There is no turning back once you embark on the mission. Trying is not an option but doing is," she said.

He shook his head in agreement. He got up and kissed his mother on the cheek. "I love you, mom. Thanks for being patient with me."

She smiled back and knew that she would spend a lot of carpet time praying for her youngest son and his bride and her new grandchild.

Chapter Twenty-Five

The day was brisk and cool but the sun shone brightly in a cloudless sky. You could see your breath in the air but the freshness gave you a clear mind. Jennifer walked out to the barn early that morning to groom her horse, Patience. She was a honey colored mare that had birthed two foals. Jennifer was given her horse by her dad on her sixteenth birthday. She fell in love with her on sight. Jennifer hadn't ridden her since her last episode with the baby. The doctor ordered her to stay off the horse as it might rupture her uterus again. Jennifer listened but she still spent time with her horse grooming and soothing her.

As she rounded the stall, she bumped into Andrew.

"Oh, I'm so sorry. Hello, Andrew. I'm surprised to see you here. What brings you to the Parker Valley Ranch?" she inquired.

"Hello, Jennifer. Jason has sent me here to talk to some of the ranch hands. What brings you to the stables? You are not going riding, I hope!" He smiled as he noticed her girth. She looked very pregnant.

"No, I haven't been riding for months now. But I miss my horse, so I come out and brush her down and talk to her. One of the hands takes her out now and then for some exercise. I can hardly wait to get back on her again. I miss being out on the range desperately."

"I can understand that." He said as he folded his arms across his chest and watched her. "How have you been, Jennifer?"

She shyly looked back at him. "I'm feeling pretty good for a pregnant girl who is about to pop in a few weeks. How have you been?" she replied awkwardly, remembering their last encounter lip to lip. She hadn't forgotten how she felt when he kissed her.

"I have wanted to come and talk to you Jennifer but I have been busy with the ranch. Can we talk sometime?" He was feeling a little uncomfortable being put in this position. "I really think we need to talk."

"Any time, Andrew. I'm home most of the time, except to go shopping now and then for Cassie. Call ahead and I will make sure that I am there." She walked away slowly. It was good talking to you, Andrew."

He nodded as she went to find her mare. He watched her waddle through the stables and he smiled. He shook away the feelings she brought up in him whenever she was around him. He wasn't sure it wasn't just a protective mechanism in him when she was around. He took a deep breath and promised himself that he would set up an appointment with Pastor Jose.

Jennifer spent the next hour talking to Patience and brushing her down. She brought her some apples and a few other treats that she liked. They playfully sought each other's company. She would nuzzle Jennifer and sniff out her pockets. Jennifer bent down and brushed her legs, when she felt two hands cover her eyes.

"Guess who?" asked a voice from behind her.

She laughed. "Let me guess! Is it Manuel? Or is it Andrew?" she teased.

"Who did you say?" he replied, a little put out. "Why would I be Andrew?"

Jealousy crept in his spirit. She rose and punched his arm. "I'm just kidding, silly. I was just talking to Andrew a little while ago. That's why his name came up. Why, are you jealous?"

"Do I have reason to be?"

"You are goofy. What are you doing here, James? I thought you were coming for lunch. It's still early yet."

"Yes, I know but I have something special to talk to you about. Will you come into the house?"

They walked out of the barn chatting small talk before they reached the main house.

Parker Valley was still in need of a lot of repairs but the outside was finished. A fresh coat of white paint and new shutters added a renewed luster to the homestead. Trees were planted around its staircase and the hominess of the spacious porch surrounding the front of the house gave it a look of sophistication.

They opened the painted double doors and entered into the warmth of the hallway. As soon as they walked in, they could smell cookies baking in the oven.

Jennifer sniffed and groaned as she loved chocolate chip cookies. "Cassie always makes cookies in the morning. I can hardly stay away from them." She stroked her stomach and spoke to her little girl. "I know you love them too don't you, little one?" She laughed.

James watched her movements and could hardly contain his love for her. He turned her around and planted a gentle kiss on her lips.

"What was that for?"

"Just looking at you stirs my heart, Jennifer, especially when you talk to our little girl like that." He smiled into her eyes. "Have you thought of a name for her yet?"

She felt comfortable in his arms. "Well I thought of calling her Angel, or Angelica."

He looked in her eyes. "And why is that?"

"It was because an angel saved her life." She answered purposely gazing back at him shyly.

He pulled her close to him and gave her back a rub. "Do you want to tell me about it?"

"Why don't we go and sit down." She agreed reluctantly.

They sat close together on the sofa and Jennifer sat facing him.

"It's probably good that we are having this conversation. I am ashamed of what I am about to tell you so please bear with me." She hung her head slightly and then looked him in the eye.

"James, there was a time when I wasn't thinking very clearly. When you left to go to the Teen Challenge Center, I found out that I was going to have a baby. I was at that time almost three or four weeks pregnant. When I watched your car drive away, I never felt so alone in my life. I decided to go back to school. Gayle, my roommate helped me get through some of the roughest times. Three weeks after that I decided to go to a clinic and have an abortion." She stopped and silently wiped her eyes as the tears fell down her cheeks.

"Oh James, I am so ashamed! I sat on the table and was going to let the doctor take my baby when the electricity went out. A person or an 'angel,' so I thought at the time, came into my room and told me to run. I used it as a sign and I ran out of that clinic as fast as I could. I felt that God was giving me another chance. I wanted so much to keep my baby and follow God's plan for my life. I knew it was an angel because I came to find out that the electricity didn't go out. It was only in my room that it happened. It must have been God." She looked at him her eyes as big as saucers.

James gulped and stiffened as he listened to Jennifer's story. It coincided with the dream he had of Jennifer lying in white sheets covered in blood. His face went white.

"Jennifer I too must tell you something darling. It was probably around that time that I had a dream about you. You were lying on a gurney covered in a white sheet.

When I looked again it was covered with blood. It frightened me so much that my roommate and I got up and prayed the whole night. It was a special time, except for the part about you. I was so frightened, Jennifer. I was so afraid something would happen to you." He leaned over and hugged her close. "Thank you for telling me. God is so good, sweetheart. I know he has a plan for our lives."

He looked at her and couldn't help but feel the presence of God.

He knelt down on one knee and took out the little velvet box he had kept hidden in his pocket. He opened it and showed it to her.

"Sweetheart, will you marry me, and be my soul mate for the rest of my life? Will you allow me to cherish and love you as long as you shall live? Will you be the love of my life until the end of time?" he asked with his heart open for all to see.

Jennifer looked at him and down at the beautiful diamond ring sparkling in the black velvet box. She gulped and started to cry.

"Yes, I would be honored to be your wife, to love and cherish you for the rest of your life. I would be honored to be your soul mate and stand by your side until the end of time." Tears rolled down her cheeks.

He took the ring out of the box and carefully placed the ring on her finger. He then picked up her hand and kissed every finger.

"You won't be disappointed, Jennifer. Thank you for allowing me to spend the rest of my life making up for causing you any pain. I can't promise that I won't hurt you again, knowingly or unknowingly. I ask you to forgive me in advance. I would never hurt you again purposely Jennifer, but I am only human. Thank you for honoring me." He cried and pulled her close and kissed her lips gently. They held on to each other for a few more minutes.

"Do you want to break the news to your sister?" he whispered in her ear.

She laughed outright and looked down at her hand. "The ring is exquisite, James. You have impeccable taste."

He just smiled and helped her up and the two of them went hand in hand to find Cassie.

News spread quickly around the ranch. Cassie was excited that the two of them had decided to marry. She felt all along that God would work out a plan for their lives. It only made sense that they would become a family and bring up their child together.

Sondra was surprised that they had become so close in such a short time. Sondra shook her head and couldn't understand how she could get something so wrong. She was sure that Andrew had fancied her sister. Perhaps he was too shy to approach her. 'Perhaps it's God's will for James and Jennifer to have a life together' she thought to herself, 'especially since they are the biological parents.'

So, accepting their marriage as the best thing for them and the baby, as a wedding present Jason and Sondra gave them tuition for their schooling at the

University James had chosen for his Seminary and day care for their little girl. James would start in the next semester and Jennifer would start full time the following semester. Meanwhile, she could take night courses and do some catch up work. That would give her time to spend settling in. The two of them were grateful for the help they would receive.

Their parents gave them an allowance that allowed them to rent a home and have enough spending money to feed and clothe them. They were excited about their new adventure together. James would continue to speak at the nearby churches and give his testimony for those who would listen. They had purpose and focus which was something he lacked in his life.

Their love grew stronger each day as they planned their life together. The wedding would be set in ten days.

Chapter Twenty-Six

Cassie and Roberta were the perfect ones to make plans for the simple family wedding. Jennifer did not want a lot of people there. She insisted that, besides family, only a few people from around the area would attend and her friend Gayle would be her maid of honor.

The total guest list was fifty people but, because of their popularity, it was growing by the minute once everyone found out. They would have a ceremony at the church and a luncheon at Willow Oaks.

Claira got busy and designed a lovely wedding dress for Jennifer. It was a simple, soft, delicate white flowing gown that was full in the waist and would hide her growing waistline. It was beautiful. Jennifer was tiny everywhere except her tummy. Only when she turned to the side could you notice her protruding middle. She laughed when she tried it on.

"Oh Claira, do you think anyone will notice?" But she did look like a lovely bride in her gown. Claira's talent went far beyond all their imagination. She could make anyone look elegant with a stitch here and there.

Her business was growing far beyond anything she could have dreamed.

'Claira's Designs' was becoming a hit with certain sectors of the Hollywood scene. It kept her busy day and night. She would sometimes be working so late that she would have to sleep at the shop. Cassie was concerned that her life was becoming too involved with the wrong crowd. She had been invited to attend the parties of some of the wildest characters in show business. First in Dallas and then a few weeks ago she was flown out by private jet to Los Angeles. Cassie worried that her innocence was too fragile for that crowd. Claira just ignored her and said it was the price you had to pay for good business.

All the weddings in the past year and the fuss made over Jennifer and her problems forced Claira to do her own thing. Jason wondered at times if she wasn't hiding away at the shop and pushing herself too hard to find her own way in life separate from her sisters. They were beginning to see less and less of her at family dinners and gatherings. Jason promised himself he would sit down and talk with her to settle his own mind. He knew what those crowds of socialites could do to you. They would draw you in and before you knew it they would suck the life out of you and spit you out without a care in the world. He wanted to protect her from that way of life as best he could. But sometimes you have to learn the hard way.

Andrew was called back into Jason's office one day and he spoke to him about the best way to protect her from that crowd but Andrew didn't know of any other way except to shadow her everywhere she went. But that would be impossible. He smiled at Jason and told him he would do everything he could to check around and find out who, and what they were and where they would hang out. He had connections in Hollywood and Nashville that would do some checking for him.

Jason was grateful and told him money was no object. Andrew nodded and said he would get right on it.

Andrew walked back to the bunk house and thought about Jennifer. His feelings for her would go unnoticed. He was actually happy that they had made the decision to get married. They would be well suited for one another and were closer in age than he and Jennifer. He wondered, if he had shown any intention towards her, if she would have considered him a suitor. He settled back and resigned himself to believe that it wouldn't have been God. He had received an answer to his prayer.

As the wedding drew closer, Jennifer started to become very uncomfortable. She was a little less than two weeks away from her delivery date and hoped that the baby could wait until after the wedding. She found it hard to maneuver and wasn't any help with the wedding plans. The guests would be arriving any day and all she could think about was sleeping. She suddenly wished that she and James had eloped. It would have been less stressful. Cassie and Tommy were troupers through all the fanfare. Jennifer could tell that Tommy was getting tired of her whining about her condition.

"Jennifer, why don't you go back upstairs and just stay out of the way," he finally spoke in anger, as he listened to her complain to Cassie for the last hour.

Her emotions were completely shot and his remark put her over the edge. She went crying out of the room and ran upstairs to her room.

"You could have been a little easier or her, darling." Cassie watched her sister leave the room crying. She was about to go after her when Tommy stopped her.

"For once, you will leave her alone," he spoke harshly to his wife. "We have enough to do and she has been asking for this for the last few days. This way we can get some work done."

Cassie frowned and looked at her husband ready to argue with him. She decided that now was not the time to debate the issue so she just shrugged her shoulders and went on with her cooking. Jennifer probably could use some alone time. She winced when she heard the door slam.

Jennifer leaned against the door and fell to her knees. She was tired of everyone telling her what to do. She was a capable young woman and wanted to help where ever she could and if they didn't want her help at her own wedding than she would just stay away. She put her head in her hands and cried silently. She sulked for the next hour. She finally fell asleep and was awakened when she heard a knock on the door.

"Who is it?" she asked.

The knocking continued. She got up out of her bed and opened the door.

"I said, who is it?"

"Hello, Jennifer," a familiar voice replied.

"Andrew? What are you doing here?" She was suddenly awake.

"I'm here to take you over to see Sondra. Your sister thought you might need some fresh company. I happened to be here and I was going over to Willow Oaks and your sister thought you might like to come with me."

"Oh she did? Well thank you very much, Andrew. Maybe I'll take some overnight clothes and stay there until the wedding. It looks like I'm not welcome here."

"Don't kill the messenger. I'm only here to escort you. I'll be downstairs and I will wait for ten minutes. If you aren't down in ten I will leave," he said. He walked away, his cowboy boots clicking on the wood floor.

"It might take me more than ten minutes," she yelled back after him.

"Ten minutes," he yelled back.

Jennifer took a deep breath and never felt so rejected in all her life. She packed her duffle bag with some night-clothes and a couple of changes of clothes. If they didn't want her here, then she would not stick around. She looked at her watch and noticed that it was almost seven o'clock. She had slept over three hours. 'Where is everyone?' she thought. It sounded like she was the only one in the house.

Chapter Twenty-Six

She quickly went down the stairs and saw Andrew waiting for her at the door.

"Where is everyone?" she asked him.

"I have no idea," he said, looking annoyed at having to wait. "Let's get going."

He opened the door and ushered her into the truck. They drove off slowly, once she had her seat belt on.

After five minutes, Andrew looked at her and smiled. "Congratulations on your upcoming marriage. I hope you will be very happy."

She looked at him shyly. "Thank you, Andrew. It was certainly a sudden decision. James really is a very special man."

"I'm sure he is."

The rest of the trip was done in silence. When they came up to the ranch, Jennifer noticed that the house was dark. She frowned slightly.

"I hope Jason and Sondra are home. I hate to just spring myself on them at the last minute," she said.

He helped her out of the car and walked her to the house. He opened the door for her and went inside to find a light. As Jennifer stepped into the room all the lights came on and everyone yelled 'surprise!' She nearly jumped out of her skin.

It was then she noticed a room full of people shouting and laughing. There were balloons and banners all over the front room. They had certainly taken her by surprise.

Sondra came over and hugged her. Cassie came over to her also and hugged her.

"I'm so sorry, Jennifer. I had to get you out of the way so we could make the sandwiches and cookies without you knowing. I know I sounded harsh. Can you ever forgive me?" she pleaded.

"Oh Cassie, I am sorry too. I must have sounded like a total brat." She hugged her back. "Thank you all for this wonderful surprise. I can't believe it." She looked around the room and it was full of people and presents.

"This is a baby shower and a wedding shower all in one. We had to do some fancy work to get this all arranged in such a short time. Claira is working late tonight so she won't be here until later."

The party was a total success. James greeted his fiancé with a big smile. "They took me by surprise too. I got here just a few minutes before you." He hugged her and held her close.

Andrew stood by the door, watching the activities with reservation. He wasn't sure whether to be pleased about the situation or not. But he did notice that they looked happy together. That was all that mattered. He would put this behind him and move on.

He turned to walk out the door when he bumped into a young woman rushing in. She was dressed elegantly in a black and white cocktail dress. Her blonde, straight, shoulder-length hair flew across her face as she turned. She had too much makeup on for his taste, and her beauty, he surmised, but with her red lips and pasty white skin she looked the part of a Hollywood Starlet.

"Excuse me," he said. He caught her as she ran into him.

"Watch where you are going!" She tried to catch herself as she fell into his arms. She looked up into his face and frowned slightly. She didn't like the feeling of being in this man's arms. His shoulders were broad and she could feel the strength in his hands as he held on to her. Instantly, he let go of her as soon as she maintained her balance.

She smoothed down her dress and pushed her hair out of her eyes. She didn't give him another thought and walked in with her five inch heels clicking through the hallway into the lovely spacious living room.

"Jennifer darling, congratulations," she said. She gave a pretend kiss to her cheek.

"Claira, you finally made it. I absolutely love my wedding gown. You are a master when it comes to design."

Andrew shook his head as he watched her go throughout the room greeting everyone. Groaning, he surmised that she was the 'designer sister' who Jason asked him to keep track of. 'God! Why me?'

The party went on for most of the evening. James and Jennifer received a lot of gifts that would help them set up their little home. Jennifer was thrilled with all the baby clothes and diapers that were given to her. She had shopped a little but didn't realize what she needed.

Tommy and Cassie gave them a crib and mattress set for the baby. It was mahogany wood with beautiful designs inlayed throughout the wood. Others gave them bumper pads and a comforter to go with them. Jennifer was over-whelmed with all the love they showed.

For wedding gifts, they received mostly money to start their new life together. James was delighted. He knew there would be hard times ahead. He was begin-ning to understand the value of money and would never take it for granted again. Hopefully, soon he could support his family on his own.

They all shared sandwiches and cake and cookies together. It wasn't until the first guests started to leave that Sondra began to feel the first twinge of labor pains. At first she thought it was a cramp but it lasted for a few minutes. She shrugged it off as indigestion until the pains kept coming throughout the rest of the evening. She decided to get up from her chair and walk around and noticed that the seat of the chair was soaking wet.

"Dear God, what has happened?" She held her stomach as the next pain doubled her over. Jason quickly came to her side and questioned her. He looked down and noticed the chair and his face turned white.

"This is it," he said out loud. He looked at Sondra and smiled. "I know it seems early but it looks like we are going to have a baby tonight."

It was Sondra's turn to go white. "I'm not ready for this. I haven't practiced enough. I can't do it, Jason."

Jason laughed and turned to Tommy. "Someone get the car started and Cassie if you will go and pack a bag for Sondra we will head off to the hospital. Someone call Doctor Martin."

"I will," one of the guests said, quickly taking charge. She was one of the nurses for Doctor Martin.

The whole room started buzzing and excitement started to build. Jennifer ran over to Sondra and held her hand.

"I'll help you anyway I can. What can I do? Jason, isn't it too early for the baby to be coming? She still has three weeks to go."

"Sometimes, these things will happen, Jennifer," he said. He ushered his wife out the door to the car. "I'm sure she will be just fine. Start praying." He turned to his wife, "Are you alright, darling?" His hand gently touched her as she doubled over in pain again.

"Oh, dear God it hurts. It's not supposed to hurt this much," she complained. Jason cringed as he watched his wife suffer.

Chapter Twenty-Seven

When they got to the hospital, Doctor Martin was waiting for them. They put her in a wheel chair and ushered her up to the maternity ward and into a birthing room. Doctor Martin had a specialist waiting to check her progress. He told Jason to wait in the waiting room until they could prep her. Jason paced the room for about half an hour until the doctor came to get him.

"We must hurry, Jason, if you want to see your son being born. She is about ready to give birth. It is a good thing you arrived when you did or your son would have been born in the car. You need to put on these surgical clothes and this mask. Wash your hands thoroughly in the sink over there. I'll meet you outside when you are ready."

Jason put on the gown and mask with shaking hands. "Dear God, take care of Sondra, and little Jacob. Only you can get us through this, Lord." He rushed out of the room and walked quickly to the delivery room.

When he got there, he heard Sondra groaning in pain. His heart flew into his chest. He ran to her side and she weakly smiled at him.

"Are you ready to meet your son?" She groaned. "Oh God, I have to push."

She was in position for delivery and the doctor urged her not to push yet.

"Breathe, darling, just breathe," he whispered in her ear. "Everything will be fine. Just think how wonderful it will be to see our baby."

"Oh Jason, I am so scared." She started shaking all over. Jason looked at the doctor with a question.

"She is in what we call 'transition,' the final stages. It's perfectly normal. Now Sondra, you can push. Push hard."

She pushed with all her might. Sweat was starting to build on her forehead.

"Okay, that was very good. Now just wait for a minute." He smiled up at her. "You are doing just fine. Okay, here we go again. Now push." Sondra pushed hard again.

Jason watched as a tiny head appeared. He stared in amazement at the life that was about to come into the world. He gulped and couldn't keep his eyes off his son.

"Okay Sondra, one more push and that shall do it," the doctor said.

She pushed one more time and little Jacob came sliding out. Jason watched in pure amazement as his son came into the world. His flesh was a pink color. The cord came out with the baby and the doctor asked him if he would like to cut it. He took the scissors and cut the cord where the doctor told him to. Just at that moment Jacob let out a yell that could be heard all over the hospital.

Jason smiled and looked at Sondra lovingly. "We have a son, sweetheart. He is just beautiful. He's perfect." A tear escaped down his cheek. "You did wonderful, darling. I'm so proud of you." He kissed her lips. The nurse had taken the baby over to the table close to them and weighed him and cleaned him off. She brought him over to Sondra and put him in her arms.

"He is six pounds nine ounces," she stated and smiled at the happy couple. "He's a good size boy for being three weeks early."

Sondra cried and held her little boy when the nurse brought him to her.

"He's just perfect, Jason. I think he looks like you," she said. A tear spilled down her cheek.

Jacob opened his bright blue eyes and looked into Sondra's eyes. He blinked and Sondra thought that he gave her a little smile. She looked at Jason and handed him over to him. Jason took his son and took his mask off and started to talk to him.

The doctor finished working on Sondra and the nurse took over. He went over to her and smiled at him.

"Congratulations. You have a fine son."

"Thank you, doctor. You did an incredible job," Jason replied.

"Your wife did all the work. I must say it was a fast delivery. I would make sure for the next one you get here sooner," he said.

The joy on Jason's face was one for the history books. You couldn't have seen a more proud father as he held his son.

Chapter Twenty-Eight

Jennifer walked into Sondra's room with balloons in one hand and a bouquet of flowers in another. Everything in the room was blue. The wallpaper was blue and the paint on the walls was light blue. Jason was sitting in the large blue room in a comfortable blue rocking chair holding the baby. Sondra was turned to one side looking at her husband hold their child. She couldn't look more content.

As Jennifer gazed around the room, it looked like a flower shop. It seemed Jason had bought out all the florist shops in the area. Jennifer self-consciously hid her pitiful bouquet of flowers behind her back but at least she had balloons.

"Well you two look quite at home. Congratulations." She went up to her bed and sat on it. "I'm proud of you, sis. It's my turn next. I hope my delivery is as quick and easy as yours was."

"Oh, Jennifer, just you wait. It was the most incredible time of my life. I won't tell you that it didn't hurt but, thank God, it was over quickly." She hugged her sister. "Did you see little Jacob? Isn't he beautiful?"

Jennifer walked over to Jason and he handed Jacob to her. She picked him up carefully and smiled into his face. He was sleeping soundly.

"He is gorgeous. You must be so proud." She stared at him for another minute and handed him back to Jason. "Thank you so much for the wonderful party last night. This was a fitting end to a wonderful day. Are you going to be alright to hold the wedding at Willow Oaks on the weekend?"

Sondra smiled. "Don't you worry, sweetheart. I am going home tomorrow and, besides, everything has been done already. Roberta and Cassie have taken care of everything. We just have to show up."

"I'm a little worried about the baby. What if she comes before the wedding? I really want to be married before the baby comes."

Sondra looked at Jason to find an answer. He just shook his head keeping his attention on his son.

"Jennifer, we will handle things as they come. You do not need to worry about anything except your wedding. It will be beautiful. You will be beautiful. We can't change what will happen. We will just pray it is exactly as God plans. Okay?"

"Okay. I know I worry for nothing. With my luck I'll be two weeks late." She laughed. "I already feel as big as a house."

"We'll be there with you, honey," she said.

Just then, the whole family showed up at the door. Jason's mother and father along with Cassie and Tommy came waltzing through the door.

"Congratulations," they cried in unison.

"Where is my grandson?" Elaine asked. She was the first to speak as she spotted Jason holding Jacob.

"Oh, my goodness, he is wonderful! Oh darling, look at you, my little precious one. I hope your daddy is taking good care of you." She picked up the baby and walked around the room. "You are so sweet. I am your grandmother and I am going to spoil you to death."

Sondra laughed at her. Watching Elaine with her son was a joy that went deep inside her spirit. She felt sad that her mom and dad would never know their grandson. It left an empty feeling inside her. She watched her husband with his father and was envious of their relationship. They were so natural together. It gave her a sense of the relationship he would have with their son. It made her feel good inside. She was content.

Seeing Sondra's baby made Jennifer believe that soon she would be holding her daughter. She sighed, wondering what it would be like. She and James would have to find a name for their little girl. She would speak to him about it tonight. It was time that she was named.

That night, she and James thought of many names that might be suitable for their daughter. The two of them sat on the sofa and discussed many. Shannon, Sharon, Liza, Bridget, Barbara, were many names that they came up with. Suddenly, Jennifer sat back and laughed.

"That's it!"

"What's it?"

"Elizabeth, Beth for short. That was my mother's name. It would honor her ,James. We need to call our daughter Elizabeth." She stood up and looked at James. "We need to do this, honey. I feel it is God's will that she be called Elizabeth. It is a name that brought me into the world. Elizabeth Nelson. It has a special ring to it, don't you think?"

James watched her dance around the room excited about coming up with a name. He wasn't sure about it but if she wanted to name their baby girl Elizabeth, then Elizabeth it would be.

"I love it, sweetheart. It is a wonderful idea that she should be named after your mother. It will keep her alive in our hearts each time we call her name. You are a genius!" he said. He held her in his arms and kissed her. He deepened his kiss as she pressed into him. She stepped back and looked at him smiling.

"I can't wait to make you my wife," he said. He pulled her back in his arms and whispered into her ear. "You drive me crazy. I love you, Jennifer. I can't wait to wake up next to you every morning."

She snuggled up to him and put her arms around him. She couldn't get too close because of her large abdomen.

"In six days I will become Mrs. Jennifer Lynn Nelson. It has a special ring to it don't you think?" she said.

"I think I better get going, Miss Parker, before I lose my dignity." He smiled at her. "Good night, my little Elizabeth, sleep tight." He bent down and kissed Jennifer's stomach. "I look forward to meeting you soon."

Jennifer went up to her bedroom. Before she went to her room, she knocked on Cassie's and Tommy's room.

"Come in," a voice said sweetly. Jennifer opened the door and peaked in.

"Hi Cassie, sorry to disturb you but I wanted to tell you the good news." She went into the room and sat down on the love seat. "We finally found a name for the baby. We are going to name her Elizabeth, after mother. What do you think?" She asked tentatively, hoping for her sister's approval.

Cassie looked at her surprised. "Why that is such a wonderful idea, Jennifer. I know mother would be thrilled." She got up and hugged her sister. "What made you think of that? I know you have struggled with a name for a long time."

"I know, but it sort of just came to me when James and I talked about names. I really miss mom, and it just popped into my head."

"I like it. 'Elizabeth Nelson.' It is a wonderful name. Good choice. Are you getting excited about the wedding?"

"I guess I'm a little nervous. So much is happening at once, with the baby and everything," she sighed.

She hugged her sister and said goodnight and went off to bed.

~

The wedding day was coming quicker than they all thought. Sondra and Jacob had come home from the hospital two days ago and they were settling in nicely. The grandparents took over a lot of the care of the baby. Elaine couldn't have been happier. It gave Sondra a chance to recover completely before the wedding.

"Oh Jason, my dress for the wedding isn't going to fit." She complained. "Whatever am I going to wear? I haven't had normal clothes on for months. It certainly will feel good." She was back down to a size six with only a little tiny tummy bulge.

The house phone rang and Jason said,

"I'll get it sweetheart." He picked up the phone and after a minute he walked out of the room in a hurry. "Is she alright?" Sondra heard him say as he left the room.

'Is who alright?' she thought to herself as she wandered out of the room after him.

She met him coming back into the room. His face was white as a sheet. The look on his face made Sondra's eyes get bigger.

"What is the matter, Jason?" She asked as fear started to creep in.

He took her arm and sat her on the sofa. He took a deep breath before he spoke.

"It's Jennifer. She and James have been in a car accident and they have taken her to the hospital. She is in critical condition. I don't know any more than that, sweetheart. We will meet James at the hospital. Let's pray before we go."

Sondra was too shocked to say anything. Silent tears poured down her face as Jason took her hand and the two of them knelt on the floor. Their prayer was a quick one.

Jason spoke to his parents and they would look after the baby. He and Sondra were in the car and on the way to the hospital before another minute passed.

The only thing you could hear in the car was the roar of its powerful engine. Sondra was praying silently as fear for her sister gripped her heart.

"Dear God, please don't let anything happen to my baby sister. Take care of the baby, Lord. She is in your hands, Father. Touch James too, Lord. He will need you most of all Father. Send your Angels to the hospital, Lord, and go before us and prepare us for what is to come. Thank you, Jesus. Thank you, Jesus. Thank you, Jesus."

She said this prayer over and over in many different ways before they got to the hospital.

~

Prayer and love were the tools this family will use for all the trials and tribulations they would go through. There would be many but, with the help of God's love for them, they would be sustained.

About the Author

Dear Reader, writing this book about date rape and what decision you make when it happens is something that has been in my heart for years. I have ministered to many women who have suffered the ill effects of drugs and rape. Each person has the ability to decide what the solution should be but I strongly suggest that you seek some Christian Counseling before you make any life-changing decisions. God is still on the throne and He instructs us in His Word to always measure the cost. Only God creates life and every life is precious. Many lives can be affected by your decision, so please choose wisely. I will pray that He guides you as He guided Jennifer.

The Parker family has gone through many trials and tribulations. It is by how we handle the trials thrown at us that we are measured. It is important to understand that, before me meet our Savior Jesus Christ, we have lived a life that is pleasing to Him. We all will make mistakes and we have a forgiving God. So, no matter what decision you have made in the past, go to the Lord and ask His forgiveness so you can have a clean slate to live a life pleasing to God.

I have written with a good friend, Varvah Allen, a counseling book titled *Heal the Broken Hearted*. If you have suffered rape, trauma, abuse, depression, anxiety, or any other adversity, I suggest that you apply the prescription from this book to your life. Jesus is the healer and He wants to heal you. To order the book, go to www.parkervalleyseries.com.

I have two children and seven grandchildren and it is with love and a strong faith that I leave them in the "Hands of the Lord." Trust in the Lord your God with all your strength and all your mind.

May God truly bless you.

PARKER VALLEY — CLAIRA
SERIES #3

Chapter One

As she stepped into the room, it was as if time stood still. Heads turned and everyone admired her beauty. She walked with confidence in her heels and stockings. Her dress flowed gently with the movement of her body. She was a breath of fresh air amongst the old Hollywood misfits and certainly looked as if she didn't belong.

Claira was surprised at how many people were in the place. It was packed with bodies, and full of smoke. The room was filled with a haze that made it difficult to see and breathe. There was laughter coming from one of the rooms in the back and she noticed that the bar was full of beautiful women and men who clung together in an almost vulgar way.

She wasn't expecting the rough crowd that seemed to be gathering. The way they looked at her wasn't giving her a very good feeling. She felt like they saw her as fresh meat. She looked around hastily for Miles. She spotted him at the bar with a woman draped all over him.

She went over to him and caught his attention.

"Darling, I wasn't expecting you so early," he said getting up from his barstool. Claira, this is Melissa. That is your name isn't it, honey?" He slurred his words.

Claira was repulsed by his attitude and wondered why she even bothered to come here tonight. She thought she was going to meet some Hollywood Stars. Miles had promised her some clients that he wanted her to meet.

She took Miles aside and whispered. "What is this place? I thought you were going to introduce me to some clients?"

"All in good time, dear. I thought we could have a little fun, sweetheart, so don't get your panties in a twist." He laughed strangely. He definitely had too much to drink. Claira felt very vulnerable.

She sat at the bar and ordered a ginger ale. Miles looked at the bartender and gave him a nod. He nodded back.

When she tasted the drink she made a face. He had put alcohol in her drink. Claira wasn't used to drinking alcohol but wanted to try and fit in. She looked around the bar and noticed that most of the people had already had too much to drink and some were smoking a funny smelling cigarette. She wasn't too naive to know it was marijuana.

Claira was feeling more uncomfortable by the minute. Most of the women were half dressed and their tops were overflowing. She gulped and had the urgency to run from this place. She didn't want to look like too much of a prude, so she stayed and drank her ginger ale, waiting for Miles to finish.

The longer she sat, the laughter got louder and the language more vulgar. "Oh God, please get me out of this," she whispered to herself. Just at that moment, she heard a loud shout coming from the back room. Someone screamed and a gun shot went off. She jumped up and started to run for the door.

People started screaming and she was caught up in the crowd. A few minutes later she heard police yelling for everyone to stay where they were. The confusion was everywhere. She didn't know where to run. Miles had already left with the woman he was with and she was left standing in the middle of the room not knowing what to do.

Just as she turned, she felt cold hands cover her mouth and drag her to the back of the bar and out the side door. She screamed and kicked as the man forcefully carried her out.

"Hush! Be quiet, Claira. We have to get you out of here." She looked up at her kidnapper and gave a small cry.

"Andrew, what are you doing here?" She looked up at his stern face.

"I'm taking care of you, so be still and quiet." He looked around making sure the way was clear, grabbed her hand and took off down the alleyway. His truck was waiting at the end of the road and he put her in it. He rode away in silence. A few minutes later he looked over at her but she stared straight ahead breathing heavily, looking like she might cry.

"I won't ask what you were doing in a place like that because I'm not your father. But since you don't have a father, what the heck were you doing in a place like that?" he inquired. The tone of his voice held a steel edge.

She looked over at him and winced, embarrassed that she would be caught in this position. "I was there to meet some clients or so I thought," she said. She was almost in tears. "The question I want to know is, what were you doing there?"

He didn't speak for a few minutes as if he was trying to put some words together. "Jason asked me to look out for you," he said. His voice became quiet. "And before you get all upset with him, it's a good thing that he did. Did you know the danger you were in? Someone was murdered in that place tonight. There were drugs, alcohol, prostitution and gambling going on in the back room. Are you that blind that you couldn't discern what was going on?" His anger was building. He was more frightened for her than he let on.

All her fears and disappointments surfaced and she started to cry. She put her hands over her face and tears ran down her cheeks. She took big gulps of air and cried out loud.

Andrew stopped the truck by the side of the road and sat there quietly until she had settled down a bit.

After a few minutes of anguish, Claira spoke softly.

"Thank you, Andrew, for being there. I was so frightened," she said. More tears flowed down her cheeks. "I thought I was going to meet some clients of Miles. I should have known better. Business doesn't come easy in this town."

Andrew chuckled and said. "You have got that one right, my dear. Perhaps I can help you out a little bit. I happen to know someone in the design business. Since I will be around, whether you like it or not, why don't we work together?"

Claira looked at him quizzically. "You know someone in the business?"

"I'm not all 'rough around the edges.' I have been around," he added. "Let's get you back to your hotel. Besides, there is some news that I am reluctant to tell you because I don't know very much." He paused as she looked at him with a question in her eyes.

"Your sister Jennifer has been in a bad car accident. Jason called me just an hour ago. I wasn't sure whether to drag you out of that place sooner but I felt I could just keep an eye on you until I heard something more permanent. There is nothing we can do except pray. When we get to the hotel we can call the hospital and find out what is going on."

Claira just looked at him stunned. "Oh, dear God, I hope Jennifer is okay. What about the baby?" she asked. Fear started creeping in. Tears ran down her cheeks. "I feel like I have been so far removed from my family. I have been so selfish with my work. I haven't paid much attention to the goings on of the family. Andrew, I'm scared."

He looked concerned too. They would wait until they reached the hotel to find out the news.

PARKER VALLEY
SERIES #3

Claira

Available at:

www.parkervalleyseries.com

Discussion Questions

1) Did you read the first book in the series *Sondra*? How has Sondra changed since finding love at Parker Valley Ranch?

2) What influence has the death of the girl's parents made on their decisions? Would their decision be any different if their parents hadn't passed away?

3) Have you ever considered abortion as an alternative to having a child? What things would be different in your life if you had made a different decision?

4) How different is your marriage to that of Sondra and Jason? Describe in detail what you would or would not change in your marriage? Has this book opened your

eyes to what your life is like now and how would you change it?

5) Would you take a friend to an abortion clinic? If so, what advice would you give her?

6) Can you identify with any of the characters in this book? Which one is like you and who do you admire the most?

7) Jesus described the marriage supper as the bride and the bridegroom going to a great feast dressed in wedding garments. How does your marriage garments epitomize the "marriage supper"? Would God be pleased with your wedding clothes?

8) Prayer was a great part of Jason's life. Is prayer an important part of your life?

www.parkervalleyseries.com